a long way from Disney

OTHER BOOKS BY SETH HARWOOD

Jack Wakes Up
Young Junius
This Is Life
Triad Death Match
In Broad Daylight
As Much Protein as an Egg
(Kindle Vonnegut World Novella)
Fisher Cat and other stories

a long way from Disney

STORIES

SETH HARWOOD

Acknowledgements

I am grateful to the following publications in which these stories originally appeared: *Charles River Review:* "When They Were Calling You In for Dinner." *Pisgah Review:* "A Long Way from Disney." *Storyglossia:* "What Happened to Everything." *Inkwell:* "Rebuilding Men." *Twenty Pounds of Headlights:* "White." *zeek.net:* "Don Flamenco's Finest Round." *The White Crow:* "This One Thing." *The Red Rock Review:* "Nilsa." *Sojourn: A Journal of the Arts:* "One of Her Good Nights." *Bayou:* "Too Early." *Ecotone:* "Walden."

I wish to express my appreciation to the Iowa Writers Workshop for its generous support. And I wish, as well, to give my thanks to Margot Welch who allowed me to live with her during the time that many of these stories were written. Finally, many thanks to my father, with whom I also lived and who helped me pay for classes and workshops at a time when I needed them.

ISBN: 0615603459
ISBN-13: 978-0615603452

For my mother, with love and gratitude.

CONTENTS

a long way from Disney

when they were calling you in for dinner

"I got his nose with the pliers," the boy said, pointing at the dog. He was explaining how he'd trained it to hunt ducks.

"I brought the duck up to give him the scent, and then I got him with the pliers," he said. He made a fist in front of the dog's snout and turned his wrist.

The dog's nose was black and shiny, it looked soft.

My family was on the Cape for vacation. The day before, we'd driven down from Boston in the car, got in late at night. The ride was long, and Mom and Dad had been quiet. Dad locked the keys in the trunk when he was unpacking.

The boy with the dog lived in one of the huts where the lights came on when Dad started yelling. It had a porch just like ours, but his was filled with old refrigerators and a couch that didn't have any cushions.

"Have you seen the creek yet?" he said.

I nodded. That morning, from our porch, I'd watched him wade in to his knees and play around in the muck.

"Come on." He led me behind the houses to where water flowed between two banks of mud. There was a bridge. He leaned over the rail and spit.

"You see those frogs?" he said. "You ever see any frogs that size?"

I shook my head. They were bigger than anything I had back home. Sometimes I found toads and long worms in our back yard, but those were always smaller than my hand—these ones were bigger than my fist.

• • •

Later, after the boy's mother had called him inside, I came back with a butterfly net. I crouched by the side of the water, my toes sinking into the mud, and dropped the net around one of the frogs. He tried to jump away, but then he was in the net and I had him.

I held the frog up to my eye-level. I could see his little toes poking through the holes in the net. His eyes were draped with clear lids that fell and then rose back up slowly. Something vibrated in his throat.

There was a big white bucket behind our cabin, and I put him in it but he jumped right out. He lay on his back, stunned, in the grass. His underbelly was whiter and smoother than the inside of my arm, but it kind of looked like the tender part just below the elbow. I set the bucket down over him and put a rock on top to hold it down.

I could hear him in there, jumping against the sides, as I walked down toward the beach.

The waves were coming up onto the sand and then rolling back down, leaving a line of foam below the seaweed. I waded in to my ankles and felt the water rush around them and the sand build up around my feet. I liked having my feet buried, and the water was cold and I liked that. I liked our summer vacation because I didn't have to go to school, or to the day camp, and I could be with my mom.

I saw the tide had come in and the sun was over on the other side of the huts, not so far above the trees anymore. Since my parents still hadn't come down to swim, I started up to find them.

My dad was yelling when I came in, but he stopped when he noticed I was there.

"Where have you been?" Mom said.

"I was at the beach. I've been waiting for you guys to come down and go swimming. You said you were going to—"

"No." My dad was shaking his head. "I still say you can't have it," he said.

Mom put both hands on the counter. She leaned over, looking down. It seemed like I was supposed to be quiet.

I could hear her breathing. She stood up and she looked at my Dad, then she started over to where I was. "What were you saying, Adam?" she asked.

"You said we could all go swimming," I said. "I was waiting. I was playing in a creek and—"

"Tell him we'll come down. Tell him we'll be there in a minute, Ellen."

I looked at my Dad. He had the toaster on the table and he was opening it up from the bottom with a screwdriver. It wasn't even ours.

"I caught a real big frog, Dad. You won't believe the size of the frogs in—"

Mom bent down and started tucking in my shirt. "Go back down to the beach now Adam, and we'll be down in a little while," she said. She turned me around to face the living room. I could see the beach and the water through the windows.

There were tiles on the floor in the kitchen—green and black ones—and the floor in the living room was wood. There were slats going sideways and the paint was starting to peel away. I was careful not to get any splinters.

Mom started talking when I got to the door, so I stopped.

Dad said, "Don't start that again! I told you already we can't afford for you to keep it!"

I went back down to the water. The sun was starting to disappear into the trees and the wind had gotten too cold to go swimming. The water looked darker. I walked up toward the other houses, and took the bucket with the frog. He looked tired, and he wasn't trying to jump out any more, but his neck was still moving in and out, so I knew he was alive.

The lights were on in the other boy's cabin, and his mother was leaning against the doorframe, smoking a cigarette. She looked at me. Their dog was chained up and the chain was taut and he was leaning his weight against it with his front paws off the ground, barking. I looked back at the boy's mother. She rubbed her cigarette out in an old coffee can and went back inside.

I walked away from the dog and ended up at the creek, out on the bridge. I leaned over the rail and dumped the frog back into the water. He wobbled a little but then he kicked and went under. He was gone.

when they were calling you in for dinner

It was getting dark but I could still see the frogs. Some of them were floating with only their eyes sticking up, and some of them sat in the mud along the edges.

I went back to the bank and found a rock. It was big, but not too heavy, and I carried it back to the bridge and balanced it out on the rail.

There was a frog floating below me. He was big, bigger than the frog I'd caught and bigger than both of my feet put together. I could see his big bubble-eyes blinking slowly and his legs were spread out behind him. The rock was flat and wide. It was heavy. I held it up over the rail, and then over the water where the frog was, and I dropped it. It made a plonk when it fell and then there was a splash that came up from the bottom of the creek. After that the water was cloudy and I couldn't see anything. Then I saw the white. I saw the color and at first I couldn't tell what it was, but then it came up and it was the frog, his pale underbody. He was floating upside-down on the surface.

I looked at the dark water and at the frog and I thought maybe the rock had just stunned him, that pretty soon he would turn over and swim away, but he didn't. He just kept floating.

I went back again and I found a bigger rock than the last one and I brought it out to the rail. I dropped that one onto the mud along the side of the creek where a frog was. It had been up on its haunches, but it hadn't jumped anywhere, and now there was just a rock sunk into the mud.

I got some more rocks and I did what I could with them, but then it was too dark to really see the frogs any more, and I had to stop. The dog was still barking back at the boy's house.

After a while, I heard someone's mother calling her kids in for dinner, and I could see it was getting late, but I stayed where I was. I stayed there standing in the middle of that bridge until the creek was only water reflecting the moon, and I could still see the white shapes along its surface.

a long way from Disney

When I was eight, my mother went to a weekend EST conference in Worcester and was never the same. Werner Ehrhardt pumped her full of ideas, broke her down and then built her from a new mold, one with new thoughts and fresh agendas. She began to believe she was a woman going places.

"I feel like a whole new being," she said, that Sunday night over dinner. "I feel like I can change mountains, dig out all of our molehills. This isn't going to stop with one weekend."

My father smiled and nodded. We were having steak for dinner and he was busy cutting my piece into eight-year-old mouthfuls. I sat quiet, looking at my mother's eyes. They were wild in their sockets, full of energy and ideas, white all around the iris so that I wondered if somehow they'd raised her eyelids where she'd been. She said, "This is so amazing Adam. This is so incredibly unbelievable! I've learned that I should no longer stand in front of the bus. That's my life; I mean this is: a bus. I know now that I'm steps away from driving it, but I have to now at least get on it and stop resisting. Here I am and I'm here so I should welcome that."

At first it was just the weekend seminars, and she did

wonderfully: she scaled the ranks of the EST system, elevating with each successive weekend, climbing through the hierarchy of the training: the diagnosing, treating and discussing of her own and others' problems. She was figuring herself into the person that she was capable of being, as Werner Ehrhardt saw it. Then there was a week-long seminar in Rochester she went away for. This left us alone in the house, my sister, my father, and me. Suddenly the rooms seemed bigger, immense even. The second floor seemed so far away from the first, and the third floor was somewhere that I didn't want to venture.

At night my father made our dinners and then, after I had watched my hour limit of TV, he tucked me in and read to me. We were making our way through The Hound of The Baskervilles, and Holmes was just discovering the hound. I liked the feeling of laying in bed with my arms pinned down by the covers and watching my dad sit close by, holding the book in his lap. There were pictures on some of the pages, and when they came to one, he held it up for me to see. That was my favorite.

I slept with a flashlight under my pillow for protection in those days. I'd try everything I could to keep my father reading, then talking, wanting him to stay, but finally he did leave, always, and he would shut the light off, and then I was alone. I'd turn on my flashlight and patrol around the walls and corners of the room with its beam, warding off monsters and hounds, whatever other demons might be lurking, fearful from Saturday afternoons watching Creature Double Feature on TV and disturbed by the horror movies they started showing once they ran out of the Godzilla movies and then Wolfman-Frankenstein-Dracula. One movie that got to me had little men coming out of the chimney and killing people in a big house. That was the one I thought of. After my flashlight patrol, I would stare directly into the light, looking at the worlds contained inside it. All it was was a bulb and a shiny cone surface around it, but looking at it from so close, I thought I could see things moving around, distinct happenings, far off places that I would someday go visit.

• • •

For my dad, Lawrence Berkman, his marriage had had its problems since well before my mom first went to EST. His hope had been that perhaps she was going through a phase, something to ignore, but when Ellen came home from work, it was as if something in the whole house had instantly changed. Most times my dad was busy at the stove making dinner—his professor's schedule left more time for cooking than her social worker's—and he waited in the kitchen to greet her. He always heard her in the hall: she would start talking to Adam, asking if he'd had a fabulous day, what he did for recess, asking what was dinner. Then she'd come into the kitchen, take Rachel out of her high chair and goo goo at her for a minute.

Other times when she came home she was tired from work and she'd just sit in the living room, drinking wine and waiting for dinner. These nights she might cry at the table. My father worried that this would scare me and he tried to comfort my mom, but usually the best he could do was to take her upstairs and get her to lie down.

At my mother's suggestion they started seeing the counselor. They met with her on Thursday nights at the building next door to where my mom worked, while a babysitter watched Rachel and me. It was at one of the early sessions that my dad first heard of his wife's family history of depression. He'd thought her family was just naturally odd, what every son-in-law had to expect from his new wife's mother and her siblings, but now it was all coming out in the terms that she usually saved for her clients. She told the counselor that her mother was manic, that her brother had been depressed on and off since college, and that her sister was already taking medication for her own manic symptoms.

"What does this mean for Adam?" my dad asked. "Does this mean our son and daughter…"

"Relax Mr. Berkman." The counselor reached out with both hands and waved her fingers at him as if she were fanning a small fire. "This isn't for you to get upset about now. Ellen has just made an important discovery."

"Do you mean that my family's manic depression might be an explanation for the way I've been feeling? For the problems we've been going through?"

My father looked at the two of them as they went on discussing the merits of this realization. "Is it possible that this kind of depression could have anything to do with someone's ability to listen?" he asked.

"Of course," the counselor said, nodding. "This has everything to do with attention when the patient is up, or on the highs as we usually say, both in terms of needing it and being able to give it out to others."

"And the lows?"

"It's similar, Mr. Berkman" she said, "But not exactly the same. When the patient is on their lows, often what we'll observe is a similar inability to listen, but a great need for attention. It will sometimes feel like they're not hearing things you tell them, but you have to continue to tell them that things are all right."

a long way from Disney

My mom was nodding, but my father hoped things weren't this clear or determined. He wanted to still be in the normal marriage he'd thought he was getting into: the one without problems or with problems that he and his wife could work out on a day to day basis—problems without clinical names. "Is this really serious?" he asked. "Do you mean this is decided then, or are there some tests that still need to be run?"

He listened to the counselor explain about manic depression for the rest of the hour and then he listened to his wife say many of the same things in the car as they drove home. He wondered how he'd gotten himself into this, but he couldn't really be mad: this was Ellen, after all, the woman he loved, and he wasn't going to abandon her just because they'd been having a hard time communicating, or because her family had a history of depression. "We can beat this right, hon?" he said, taking her hand out of her lap and holding it in his own.

"Sure we can," she told him. "I think."

• • •

It was after the weeklong EST seminar in Rochester that things really started to change for my mom. When she got back, the house and the things in it seemed smaller. My father was still a good husband, but now he seemed merely dependable and consistent, rather than exciting and engaging, like a man she'd love. She began to find problems in almost everything he did: the way he read his book at night in bed, holding his glasses; the way he offered the same options every day for breakfast—"hot cereal, cold cereal, eggs, toast…"— the way he drove when he picked her up for work: meticulously and carefully, with great care, listening to classical music on an AM station.

She wondered if she could have done better. Not just in

terms of a better man, but she wanted to know if she belonged in a better life. Whether her life's path was or was not supposed to contain my father became almost a constant obsession. She began to look for signs of whether they were intended for each other. Werner Ehrhardt had told her that she was destined for incredible heights if she could only listen to her destiny and follow it. At work she closed her eyes at her desk and tried to listen for her life's intention. She doubted if it was supposed to involve working at a desk, but when she saw clients she knew she was on the right track: there was something definitely right about her ability to talk to people. She knew she was intended to help them.

My mother tried to listen to the little things that came into her life. Depending on whether she got quarters or combinations of coins when she bought things—her breakfast or lunch, a magazine, clothes at Filene's Basement—she judged whether she was on the right track. If she got quarters only, she could put those into the front-pocket of her wallet. That was where she kept quarters for her vending machines at work, or the money that she would consider acceptable to give a cashier—her mother had taught her that paying for something with nickels and pennies only took up too much of someone else's time. Occasionally she would put dimes into the pocket of her purse along with the quarters, but only when she got dimes and quarters as change, or dimes alone. Any combination that featured pennies or nickels she removed any quarters from and dumped the rest into her purse. Every other week or so, when she had some time and she remembered, she would remove the intended objects of her purse—her business card holder, lipsticks, make-up, tissues, her wallet—and she would dump out the rest of the change into a drawer in her desk. After picking out the garbage items, the stray gum wrappers and unwanted receipts, she left the coins in the drawer, her inappropriate coin collection.

Part of her believed every penny in the drawer held some indication that her life with my dad wasn't fated. This seemed only partly rational, and somewhat unrealistic, but still in some way she believed it. She asked herself if she really believed any of this sometimes, knew one couldn't go around deciding her life based on coin-collecting, but—and there was always this contradiction in her mind—she felt she needed to listen very hard to the world and all of the things around her, that there would be messages that came into her life from outside her, from her surroundings.

Sometimes, in-between clients, she would sift through the coin drawer and examine the pennies it held. She looked for the older ones, or the new ones, trying to see if she could find any information in the pennies that had come into her life. If she found a nice one, she asked herself what had she done in that year? Was this before or after her relationship with my father had started, and how productive had that year been? She considered all of this as information directed toward her, intended for her consideration.

When the treasury started minting the new John F. Kennedy fifty-cent pieces, my mother knew she was really onto something. These were bright new coins that she could pay with. They were shiny and large and they paid tribute to a great man in America. There was nothing inappropriate in using them, she was certain, and she even found pride in paying for her coffee in the morning without any bills. The fact that this new coin came about at the time she was most interested in change seemed altogether meaningful. It seemed irrefutable evidence and confirmation that her listening to the world around her was going well, that she was definitely onto something. EST, the way she was thinking about my father, what she and Werner knew were the right directions for her life, all of these had to be leading her along some kind of path. She wouldn't go on looking at coins for the rest of her life, she realized, but she knew to keep listening, that something was going to happen soon, or was happening already for a reason.

About this time, Werner Ehrhardt announced that another week-long seminar would be taking place that summer, in Rochester, and this time participants' families were not only invited, but were strongly encouraged to come along.

• • •

On the way to Rochester for the EST conference, we stopped off in the Berkshires to stay with some friends of my parents, the Mirkins. Their house was a big one on a big lake, and the Mirkins had planned a barbeque for our arrival. They had two daughters, one a few years older and one a few years younger than me. They made me nervous: the way they talked in whispers, or scrutinized me like they would paint me all over, as if they needed to decide on a particular color for each part of my body. And they loved and adored Rachel. As soon as we arrived, they took her away and started dressing her in their old clothes.

In the car my parents had been quiet. Coming through Worcester my mother had said something that had made my father stop talking, then for the rest of the way they hadn't spoken. My mother made periodic stabs at the car radio buttons and these were the only movement in the front. Once, when they got off the turnpike, my dad pointed to the directions on her side of the car. She had raised her palms as if to show him and said, "You know this is what I've been thinking. You know these are questions I want to deal with." But he had merely raised his hand to the side of his face as if it were a blinder, and continued driving. "The directions, Ellen," he said. "Please. Just the directions."

So it was a choice of one discomfort over another that led me into the lake with the Mirkin sisters instead of staying close to my parents that afternoon. I followed the girls down the hill to the shoreline after we'd eaten, nervous about being alone with them, but eager to swim in the clear water. The younger one, Stephanie, dropped her clothes to reveal a pink one-piece with frills around her shoulders. Her stomach protruded beyond all her other parts, a rounded pink globe. Rachel had on her yellow bathing suit. She waddled into the water with Stephanie, the two of them moving together, Rachel with her orange water wings holding Stephanie's hand.

I watched Jane. The first thing she did was unfasten her shorts. When she did, I thought I could see her belly button and when they fell to the ground I saw the bottom of a black two-piece bathing suit. Then she raised her T-shirt over her head, and I saw the bikini completely. It was the first time I'd seen one up close, or really been around a girl's body like that; I could see her flat, tanned belly, her legs, and the fact that she had a reason to be wearing the top.

"Aren't you going to take your shirt off?" Stephanie said, splashing water at me from the edge of the lake. Jane laughed. She dropped her shirt onto the sand and ran into the water.

Turning, I saw her back, most of it, her black hair hanging down just past her shoulders, and her shoulder blades raise as she lifted her arms to dive into the water. She began a perfect crawl away from me, out into the water toward the float.

I lifted my shirt over my head and held in my stomach. Somehow I'd put on weight in the last school year. While I'd been thin a year ago, a new candy store had opened on my way from school to the bus in the afternoon. My school had stopped the funding for a school bus and now we had to take the T. The temptation of a drawerful of quarters for the bus and the candy store on my route proved too much. And these daily indulgences had added something to my body. I looked down at myself and pulled my stomach in, then started into the water, where I thought I could hide. I plodded into the cold until it reached my knees and then I dove in. When I came up I heard a noise that I thought at first might be my own screaming, that I might actually be yelling about the cold. But then I saw Stephanie and Jane's faces. The noise hadn't come from me; they were looking up the hill toward the house.

I turned to see my mother standing next to the others with her arms raised over her head. She was yelling. I was too far away to hear what she said, but she was yelling and pointing at my father. The way my father kept his head down, as if he were just looking at his hands, rubbing them together, and the way the Mirkins tried to pacify my mother—first his, then her hand reaching out for her shoulder—and then pulled back, nodded to each other and went into the house, I could see it all. My mother gestured wildly, waving her hands and saying something that looked as if she repeated it again and again. Finally, my father looked up and spoke, but my mom didn't stop to listen.

a long way from Disney

"What's going on?" Stephanie asked, standing next to me.

"They're fighting," Jane told her.

• • •

My father had known that my mom was headed for a breakdown when they'd been in the car, that it was only a matter of when. Now, in front of their friends, but luckily away from the children, Ellen had gone into this: her belief that she needed to be out of this marriage, that somehow he and the kids were holding her back. Whether this was her own manic high-side or something Werner Ehrhardt had pumped into her, he had no idea. She said she was meant to accomplish much more than she could within what they were and she needed to get out of their marriage altogether.

"OK," he said, "I'm not going to fight you anymore. I'm not going to fight your decisions for your life."

"But you know that this is right for me! You know it!"

My dad looked down at his hands. It seemed they should be scarred from the fights he had had with her over all of this, but they weren't. They were just simple hands, the hands of a man who had lived with the Wanji in Tanzania for two years and once dug ditches with them to set traps to catch the birds they would eat, pink hands that could hold his daughter, but could only pull on the things around him—his wife and his marriage—so hard, hands that had to sometimes let go.

"I'm telling you I don't want to fight you about this anymore," he told my mother. "I'm saying that you can have what you want. You have to do what you need with your life."

• • •

From the water, I saw my father get up from sitting on the picnic table and walk across the lawn, then open the back door and disappear into the house. My mother sat down on the bench of the table, next to where he had been, and put her face in her hands. Although I couldn't see her face, I noticed the movement of her shoulders, the way they jiggled up and down.

"Don't you want to go out and see if your parents are all right?" Jane asked.

"No." I looked down at my hands: they had become pruney from the water, but I didn't care. My stomach was out, above the water.

"Let's swim," Stephanie said, and then she took off with Rachel flapping and kicking in tow. Jane headed out toward the raft, swimming her beautiful crawl.

I stayed where I was. I could feel the dirt and leaves under my feet and the funny way my fingers felt when I rubbed them against my thumbs, the wrinkles bumping against each other, fitting together and then not fitting at all.

• • •

My father watched us carefully as we stayed on at the Mirkins' without my mom. She had gone on to Rochester, on the bus, and he'd arranged to pick her up at the end of the conference, when she was ready to drive back to Boston. She'd said she would call, that driving back to Boston might not necessarily be what she'd want.

I noticed that my father stayed quiet a lot now, and took swims in the lake by himself. When he spoke to me, he seemed happy, like he was trying to keep everything fun, but I could see in the corners of his eyes that things were different. I couldn't place exactly what was different until one night when my father was tucking me in. When he gave me a hug, I felt the scratch of his unshaven face against my own, and saw that my father had started squinting. A tired look had come into his eyes, not in the wrinkles that were starting to form around the edges, or in the eyes themselves, but in the way he held them open. I hugged him around the neck and tried to hold on, to keep him sitting on the edge of the bed.

"Don't go downstairs now, Dad. Stay up here for a while, OK?"

My father took my arms in his hands and freed his head from my grasp. He nodded and put his hand onto my chest. "How would you like to go for a trip this week?" he asked. "We'll go somewhere and have fun."

"Where will we go?"

My dad shook his head and patted my chest. "I guess I'll tell you in the morning."

"But don't go yet. OK, Dad? Stay here for a little while and help me sleep." Whatever light had come into my father left again. "How about we could drive to Disney World, Dad. That would be fun."

He laughed. "Disney's a long way. I'll think of something, though. In the morning we'll figure it out." He stood up. "I'll leave on the hall light for you."

My father turned the light off next to my bed and walked to the door. When he opened it, I said, "Dad?" The hall seemed very bright. He turned back into the room, closed the door all but six inches.

He tried to sound strong, to keep his voice happy and

pleasant and adult for me—they'd decided it was best not to tell us all of the details just yet—but he didn't: something got caught in his throat and he had to cough before he could say, "Adam?"

"Nothing, Dad. It's OK, now. It's nothing."

He opened the door again. From the light in the hall he could see my head on the pillow, my eyes squinted tight-shut against the oncoming tears. My father returned to the bedside and put his hand on my arm. When I sat up, crying, and buried my head in his chest, he held me.

"It'll be all right," he said. "One day soon. It'll be all right."

"What happened with you and Mom, Dad? Why didn't we go with her?"

"Your mother feels like she might need some changes right now, and if we're going to help her at all we've got to let her see them. She needs to do some things on her own."

"Is she coming back?"

"She is," my dad said. "I think."

In the morning he told me he was leaving to go on to Rochester. I looked up from my cereal. "You're going to find Mom?"

"I don't know. I just mean I'm going to Rochester." He stood up, nodded at me, and left the kitchen. I ran to the window to watch him. Rachel stayed in her high chair, Jane and Stephanie feeding her toast. Finally my dad came outside. He walked down to the lake, stood next to the water. I watched him pick up a rock and skip it across the lake. Then he did it again. I rushed through the rest of my cereal and ran down to the shore to skip rocks with him.

"What's happening, Dad?"

a long way from Disney

"I don't know if your mother is going to want to come home with us," he said.

I looked at him, and he looked away, out at the water. "Are you getting divorced?" He looked at how the trees met the sky far ahead of him: thin clouds stretched over them in horizontal lines that gave a sense of the sky's enormity.

"We have to talk more. That's what we need. I'm going to see what I can say."

"But I thought we were going to Disney."

"Disney's a long way, Adam. A long way away from Rochester."

• • •

When he had packed all of his things into the car, my father headed west for Rochester. He drove out of Massachusetts and into New York State, listening to whatever classical music he could find on the radio. He tried to hum whatever music he needed in his own head. It was a clear summer day and tall, green trees bound the highway on both sides. On the other side of a median, he could see the traffic headed back east, toward Boston, but sometimes he drove through tall trees on both sides of the highway and felt as if he was passing through a huge woods, driving by himself in the wilderness, with only the one direction available. Occasionally he passed parts of blasted-away hillsides, or slight mountains that appeared as flat cliffs, ridged with the drilled holes that road-makers had packed dynamite into to explode away the earth.

In Rochester, the most he could get my mother to consent to was talking over dinner. That was the longest she would leave her conference. Before they were to meet, he put a tie on, though the restaurant wasn't fancy, and went downstairs to the lobby to wait. In the elevator down, he straightened his tie in his reflection on the polished brass doors. He hoped that Rachel and I would do all right at the Mirkins', knew it may not have been right to leave us, but that it didn't make sense for us to be around whatever he and my mother had to say, or whatever she would do, and so leaving us had been the only option.

The lobby of the Sheraton was a big one, perhaps the biggest and fanciest that Rochester had to offer. My dad walked around in it, feeling it out, but he didn't see my mom. He took a large chair on the side of the room where he could see the door to the main hall, where he supposed the late-afternoon EST session would be happening. He could hear clapping from inside, and then more, and he hoped things would be wrapping up soon.

Their therapist had said that patience and understanding were the best things he could give his wife, that he needed to listen and offer her everything he could. A waitress came over to ask if he'd like a cocktail, and he declined. When she'd gone, he wondered if that'd been the right thing, if he could've had something to warm up to this conversation, or if being loose was even a good idea at all. He decided he really didn't know.

A mother walked into the lobby leading a small boy by the hand. She walked him to the reception desk, where she spoke to the concierge. The boy dug with both hands in his pockets. He brought out something that he at first picked at, then began to put into his mouth. His mother slapped it out of his hand just as it reached his lips, and whatever it was dropped on the floor. She held his hand in hers and slapped it. "Justin!" she said. "Don't eat that!" She went back to talking with the concierge as the boy stooped to pick up what he'd dropped and then put it back into his pocket. My dad wondered again about his kids.

a long way from Disney

What was the best way to take care of us? What kind of upbringing? It made the most sense for us to have two parents, for both of them to love each other, for them to live together and take care of us. That much seemed clear.

The big doors of the meeting hall remained closed.

My father stood up and looked around the lobby. It seemed that no one had noticed him. There was a man and a woman, sitting on a couch, drinking from martini glasses and reading the newspaper. A young couple walked in and waited at the desk behind the mother and her child. My father approached the porter, a young man dressed in a red uniform standing by the doors.

"Do you know when the conference in the main hall will finish?"

"No, sir." The porter shook his head. "In a few minutes perhaps."

My dad nodded. "Thank you." He walked to the side, toward the doors of the hall, regarding them. He thought he could still hear clapping from within, and behind that a strong male voice. It seemed as if a great meeting was happening within the conference center, that something was occurring which he should be a part of, but wasn't. He could hear the applause inside, loud and clear, obviously encouraging whatever great insight had been spoken. He moved closer, so that he was standing next to the crack between two of the doors, and leaned against them to listen.

"Your life," the male voice said, "is nothing if not a series of decisions, ones you can make every day. Ones you have to. From there whatever you decide, it becomes you." There was an interruption of applause. "It's up to you, then, working with us, to fulfill what you want of that life! To get the most out of every day possible. For you! This isn't about all the others, the ones who are there. This is about us here, in this room. How can we get—"

My father leaned away. The applause began again. He watched the porter walk outside. The newspaper readers had not looked up. My father felt as if no one in the world might know he existed. He thought he could slip inside the doors and join the meeting. He could go along with them and find out what he had coming, find how he could go get it, whatever it was as far as he was concerned, that he needed to make himself whole.

But when he opened the door he heard the waves of applause begin again as if anew, and looking inside he saw the audience standing. He saw them all rise and the single man above them on the stage hold his arms in the air and smile into the applause, nodding. He slipped into the room along the wall. A woman a few rows away from him turned and noticed him despite her fervent clapping. She stopped and regarded him seriously. She wore a name badge and the woman next to her and the man in front of her did also. The woman turned back to the stage and resumed her clapping.

My father turned to look at the stage again, saw Werner Ehrhardt, the man whose face he'd seen on the backs of my mother's books, smiling broadly, nodding. "My friends," he said, quieting them with a downward gesture of his hands. "We thank you all for coming. And I ask you, Are you ready to seize what you have belonging to you? What rights and opportunities are yours? Because what we've done today, this weekend, is help to make you realize that, I hope. No. I am sure. I—"

a long way from Disney

That was when my father saw my mother in the crowd. He saw her face reverently pointed up toward the stage, her eyes full of understanding and peaceful quiet. She was nodding, and she had her hands clasped in front of her chest, poised and ready to begin clapping all over again. And he knew that she would continue with this track in her life, that she believed this man and would follow him for as long and to wherever it took for her to get what she wanted, what she thought she had coming and deserved in this life, whatever that might be.

And he wondered if he should stay, listen and consider what he might become with the help of these systems, or if there was something he was meant to achieve, something he was meant to be. At the same time he knew that he did exist already: to some people, the ones who were important to him, and if not at all times, then at least every day. Every day he was a part of his son's and his daughter's lives, a father to two children. If that wasn't a meaning, then he didn't know what was.

He looked around one final time and made his way out of the hall and away from it, across the lobby toward the revolving glass doors of the hotel. He passed through them and walked outside. He went past the young couple that was now helping the porter unload their car, and he didn't stop; he walked into the streets of Rochester, into the cold night. He would simply go on walking, he decided, and when he came back he would go upstairs, pack his things, and return to the Berkshires to be with his son and daughter. He would make sure then that my sister and I were all right.

what happened to everything

The schedule is this: we go to my mom's house for dinner on Monday but don't sleep over, sleep over after dinner on Thursday night with Mom driving us to school on Friday morning, and the weekends rotate: first weekend we stay Thursday, Friday, Saturday, second is Thursday, Friday, third just Thursday, and fourth goes back to Thursday, Friday, Saturday, with the day on Sunday.

But Rachel and I go to school in Newton, where my dad lives. Always school and homework at Dad's, no more than two hours of TV a day, and bedtime is ten; Mom's is where I watch as much TV as I want and go to bed whenever.

In the summer my mom takes us swimming at her friend's pool in Weston. Her friend's kind of old and has a husband in a wheelchair, so why they have a swimming pool, I'm not sure. I guess you don't get rid of an in-ground pool once you have one. But Mrs. Bartley talks all kind of therapy stuff to my mom, while I try not to listen. I like swimming there better than the town pool because usually no one's there but us. They even have a diving board, which doesn't have the spring of the town pool's. But still.

what happened to everything

After the pool we stop at McDonald's. My sister and I get Chicken McNuggets, each of us a six-piece, then I started getting the nine. Now they have a twenty-piece size that we share, sitting in the back seat. She still can't eat more than six, so the twenty-piece means more for me.

This time the line at the Drive-Thru is way backed up, so my mom parks. "We're going to have to go inside this time, troops," she tells us.

It's hot in the car but we're listening to the Top-40 Countdown on the radio. "But I need to hear the Top Five songs," I say. "What if Safety Dance is Number One and I miss it?"

"Come on, Adam. We're going in."

"But it's at song four right now." She shuts the car off and I get out barefoot to follow her and Rachel across the hot tarmac and inside the McDonald's. Luckily it's nice and cool inside in the air conditioning.

All summer, "Safety Dance" by Men Without Hats has climbed through the Top Ten but it hasn't made it to Number One yet, even though it's obviously the best song. For some reason, the Number One Song has been "Take On Me" by A-Ha for the last three weeks, and "Safety Dance" has been stuck at Number Two, but that can't stay. For three countdowns they've been like that: one and two, only in the wrong order. Eventually "Safety Dance" has to hit Number One because it's the best song. It has to.

"We'll be back for the countdown," my mom says. "This will take five minutes." But we can both see that the lines are long. Several lines lead back from the front registers and add to a pile of people standing in the center of the McDonald's.

Besides getting us McDonald's, another good thing about my mom is that she lets us listen to good music in the car. She lets me put the radio on my stations that play my music, and she even likes it. She buys good albums like Flashdance and she just got Thriller and Duran Duran. With my dad it's all classical music and boring stuff; he complains if we ever listen to what I like.

"We should've used the Drive Thru," I say.

My mother looks down at me and says nothing. Rachel takes her thumb out of her mouth just long enough to say, "I have to go to the bathroom." She hangs on my mother's arm, practically pulling her down.

"I'm standing in the line now, honey," my mother says. Then she looks at me. "Why don't you take her to the bathroom, Adam?"

I look around but nobody seems to have heard how crazy this is. "I can't take her," I say. "She needs the girls'."

My mom looks down at Rachel, who is still sucking her thumb, her eyes glassed-over like she's beaming in something from way out in space, a station that no one but she can hear, like she's not even in the McDonald's. She sits down on the tiles.

"Mom," I say. "I don't think it's a good idea for her to be sitting down in here."

My mother moves up a space in the line. She rubs her hand over her face. "Can you watch your sister, please."

Mom's wearing a blue and white bathing suit, the kind with flowers on it. It's got a little skirt that hangs down from her middle, but here in the McDonald's, the skirt doesn't even come down to the bottom of her butt. In the pool, it flows around her, but here? No. I see two boys, sitting by the front window by themselves. They're sucking their straws and laughing. One of them looks at me and I turn away. I wonder how they got here, how they get to go to McDonald's without their parents, how they'll get home. I hope they're not laughing at me but I know that it's not cool to be in here like this, with my mom and Rachel. I'm wearing my yellow bathing suit, which's gotten too tight, and I'm growing out of my old computer camp T-shirt.

My mom's still not getting up to the front of the line. "We should've just gone to another McDonald's that has a Drive Thru," I say. Rachel's on the floor, sucking her thumb, disturbing where the line would be filling in behind my mother. I pull her arm to get her up. "Stand up, Rachel. Now. Come on."

She just whines and lets me pull her up so that we're both standing behind my mom. "I have to go to the bathroom," she says, stamping her feet. She's only five this summer, a few months from six. She wears a yellow bathing suit, her tummy poking out in a big round circle. Not that it's a big belly, but it is round. "Can you see your feet from there?" I ask her. She's got her thumb in her mouth as she bends over and looks. She nods her head.

"What are we getting?"

"Twenty piece McNuggets, two sweet and sour sauces, one BBQ," I say. "One Sprite, one orange." We move up one space.

"Rachel?" Rachel looks up at my mother like she's about to start crying. There's always something wrong with her, no matter where we are. One time, in the car, she tried to head-butt me and hit the top of my head with her nose. She got a nose-bleed from it and my mom got mad at me. Why? I have no idea. "Do you want McNuggets?" my mom asks. Rachel nods.

"I have to go to the bathroom."

Mom's weight shifts from one foot to the other. "Adam, can you take her?"

"No," I say. "I can't go in there."

"Can't you just take her into the boys'?"

"She can't go in the boys', mom."

My mom lets out a big puff of air. "Can you just wait two minutes, Rachel? Mommy can't get out of the line right now."

Rachel sits down on the floor again. This is when I realize that my family is one of freaks and that I'll never amount to anything. We can't even get through the McDonald's without causing a scene. I don't want to look at the boys in the front, see what they're saying now, and I don't want to see where I am either.

My mom starts looking through her purse and I can hear the person two ahead of us ordering two six-piece McNuggets, a Big Mac, and three medium cokes. He orders two medium fries also, and this is when I see the water starting to spread away from my sister across the floor. She's not really doing anything, just sucking her thumb, as far gone as ever, but now she has a puddle forming on the side of her closer to me. At first it grows on the brown tiles and then it pools and starts moving toward me along the off-white cracks between the tiles. I watch it build up speed and start moving back down the line, headed for the little metal grate at the middle of the McDonald's. For a while, I'm just watching this, not believing it, seeing this stream head away from us. Then I hear someone laugh and I back away from the trickle, bumping into a lady who says, "Excuse me."

"Oh my gosh," someone says.

"Mom," I say, tugging on the skirt of her bathing suit.

"What, Adam?" She turns around. "What is it now?" I just point at Rachel, who starts crying. "What did you do?" my mom asks. Rachel's mouth is warped into an awful grimace around her thumb, her chin all wrinkled. I step away from the crack with the pee running along it, and now the puddle covers two cracks and runs down both of them in parallel. It kind of seeps into the horizontals along the way, spreading across the floor but not going anywhere. The biggest puddle is still under and just next to Rachel.

"She peed," I say. I point at her, and the skin on my arms starts to tingle, almost hurt. A boy in a yellow and white shirt laughs and covers his mouth. He's not older than Rachel. His mother takes his head in her hands and faces him toward the front of the line, but he turns toward us again, his eyes wide. My mom picks Rachel up, not even worrying about the front of her bathing suit.

"Gross."

"Oh, baby," my mom says, patting Rachel's head.

Now the puddle is alone on the floor, taking up about a six-tile area, three by two. The trickles still head toward the grate, only now the lines of people have opened up a space around them. I can feel my face burning with eyes but I don't look up to see the stares. I look down, see my big toes, wish I had shoes on, sandals at least.

I turn and start for the door, the back of the line, not even saying anything to my mother or looking back at Rachel. I just look down, watching the white lines between the tiles until the trickles hit the grate and then I watch the dry lines all the way to the door, trying my best not to hear the two boys at the front laughing. I push through the heavy door and out into the thick, hot air of the summer.

When my mom comes out, she's carrying my sister but not any McDonald's. Rachel's still crying, and my mom looks tired, not like she's mad at Rachel, which she should be, but just tired. She puts Rachel in the back seat, on a towel, and takes down the straps, then pulls off Rachel's whole bathing suit. She sits her up and buckles the seatbelt around her.

"What about McDonald's?" I say, and my mom just gives me a look that says it all. By the time she gets the car started, Rachel has her thumb in her mouth again and she's quiet, tuned out. The radio plays the second and third verses of "Take On Me" and when it ends, Casey Kasem comes on and says it was Number One again and now that's four weeks straight and isn't it a great song. "I didn't hear 'Safety Dance,'" I tell my mom, in a voice so small she doesn't hear it. If she does, she doesn't answer. She drives us out of the lot and turns right, taking us toward home.

• • •

Rachel sleeps in the back seat the whole way. There's a spot right in front of our house and my mom parks on the street. She hasn't parked in the driveway since she pulled out with the door open and bent it back against a tree so bad it wouldn't close anymore. That was an awful day. My mom just lay down on the porch of our house and cried, stomping her feet on the wood. We had to tie rope around the car later to keep the door closed so we could take it to get fixed. Now she gets out of the car and walks around to the trunk, opens it and takes her big bag with our towels out of it. "Come in and get some food, Adam," she says, heading toward the house.

She lives in the bottom half of a two-family on Huron Avenue that she rents from a friend she met at EST—the same place she met Mrs. Bartley, the lady who owns the pool. This is where she gets all her ideas about life, and what to do with it, how she decided to leave my dad. Now those people are her friends. They're rich.

Rachel lies on her side on a towel. She's naked. Huron Ave. isn't busy, but people walk by. "What should we do with Rachel?" I ask.

My mom looks back. "Let her sleep," she says, waving her hand. "She'll be fine."

I'm hungry, but it seems weird to leave Rachel in the car naked. We're right out on the street, with the sidewalk right here, and anyone could see in. But my mom's already gone up the steps into the house, so I take one last look at my sister sleeping on her side with no clothes on. She has her legs together, her knees into the back of my mother's seat and you can't see too much. Still though, she's naked.

I roll down my window a bit and then make sure that all the doors are locked and that her window's open a little so she can get some air. She looks peaceful, sucking her thumb. You can see her bare chest though. I get out, making sure to lock my door, and head inside.

"What do you want to eat? Spaghetti O's, Boyardee Raviolis?" A pan bangs onto the stove and a cabinet door slams in the kitchen.

"Are you sure it's a good idea to leave Rachel out in the car?"

My mom comes into the hall. "She'll be fine. Come eat." She has the can of ravioli open and when I follow her in she starts banging it against the frying pan on the stove. The stove in her apartment is old and you have to light a match to get it going. She does, then when the gas comes on it pops, hisses, then it's lit. The whole apartment is old; nothing has been changed here for a long time, but it's OK. Except for the nights it's too hot and my mom and I have to sleep in the same bed, next to the big fan.

"If we had McNuggets—"

"We're not having McNuggets." My mom looks at me. She still wears her bathing suit but has a real skirt pulled up around her waist now. "No more about the nuggets, Adam, please." She turns back to the stove. There's a quiet sizzle coming from the pan.

"I think we should go check on Rachel. She's naked out there."

"She's fine," my mother says, and this time she's more definite when she says it, like she doesn't want to say it again. She's shaking her head. I get up from the table as quiet as I can. When I look back from the kitchen doorway she's got her hand up to her face, pressing her eyes with her thumb and her first finger.

From the living room I see our car on the street, with a man walking by it. I walk out into the front hall and cross the

34

rug to the door. Through the screen I see Rachel's bare foot bottom pressed against the window glass. I have to go outside. Through the door, across the porch and down the steps, the closer I get to the car, the more of Rachel's leg I can see in the window. I see the back of her thigh, its pale pink flesh and when I get onto the sidewalk, close enough that I can see into the back seat, I see her naked, laid out on her back now, nipples exposed and with one leg up and the other down on the floor so that anyone can see in between.

I try the handle but the door is locked. "Rachel," I say, hitting the glass with both hands. Her hand moves only to press her thumb farther into her mouth; she does not stir, either to put her leg down or to cover herself. "Rachel," I yell, hitting the window harder now, with the bottoms of my fists. She only rolls over, onto her side, but doesn't wake up. I try to reach in through the window to unlock the door. I only left it open a few inches, and the lock button looks far away, but by wriggling and squeezing, I get my arm in up to the elbow, and then by stretching up onto my toes, I manage to get it in up to my armpit. I get my finger onto the lock and, after scratching at it a few times, I manage to get a hold on it enough that it slips up and unlocks. I open the door just as Rachel's starting to wake up and look around.

She opens her eyes and looks at me, dazed from the sleep and the heat, her thumb out of her mouth. She's got the seat-lines marked into her face and her arm. Her hair is matted onto her forehead with sweat. "Come here," I say, taking her hand to pull her toward me.

She bends her knees and I run my arm underneath them to scoop her up. "Rachel, come here baby," I tell her, and she puts her hands onto my shoulders. "We're going inside now," I say as I lift her.

She's heavy, but I manage to stand and hold her small naked body to my chest. Her fingernails scratch my shoulders through my T-shirt. I kick the car door closed.

"Leave me down," she says.

"I'm taking you inside."

"Leave me down!"

I drop Rachel's legs and bend to let her feet hit the ground, and then I take her hand and we run up the steps of the front porch and into the house.

From the kitchen, my mother calls, "What's going on out there?"

"Nothing." I lead Rachel toward her room. Hers is the room across the hall, the one that doubles as my mom's office— where she sees clients. Rachel sleeps on a fold-out bed but has her own dresser. "You need clothes," I say.

Her thumb is in her mouth again and she looks up at me with those distant, glassed-over eyes.

"Adam, your raviolis are ready."

As I hold a pink T-shirt up over Rachel's chest, my mom appears in the doorway. "Why did you wake your sister?" She comes over and scoops Rachel into her arms and smooths the hair off of Rachel's forehead. "If she's sleeping you can leave her sleeping."

"We couldn't just leave her out in the street like that."

My mom tilts her head at me and shifts Rachel around

onto her other hip. I see Rachel's face, the far-gone eyes over her nose and hand, and below that the red nipples over her round white belly. "You sound like your dad, Adam. She's a little girl; no one's hurt by it.

"Just sit down before your food gets cold." She says, pointing toward the kitchen. She takes Rachel into the living room. "Are you hungry?" I can hear her saying, and then she calls back that I should save some of the raviolis for Rachel.

"OK." I go into the kitchen and see the raviolis on the table. I don't let them cool by cutting them in half, I just blow on them, then fork them in and chew with my mouth open, blowing out so it doesn't burn. When I hear my mom coming, I put one into my mouth right off the plate, without blowing on it, and when it hits my tongue it's so hot I have to spit it out. I clap my hand to my mouth the same instant I see my mom come into the kitchen. The top of my mouth feels like it's dripping skin-pieces, like I just burned myself on hot pizza, and some part of my arm I wasn't even thinking about hits my plate—just tips it really!—and the whole thing falls over the edge of the table. I see the rest happening like slow motion: the raviolis hit the floor, making a wet sound, the plate bounces, sort-of, and starts to rattle around in a circle, rolling itself flat, but I catch it before it falls completely. The raviolis lie spread across the floor. I look up at my mom, holding the plate for her to see it's not broken, but she's staring at the floor, not smiling.

"Jesus, Adam," she says. She shakes her head. "I leave you alone for one God-damned minute." She hits herself on the leg, hard, it looks like. "Damn it!" she yells. She walks out of the room, goes into Rachel's, and slams the door. She opens it again, re-slams it.

"Shit," I say under my breath. "Shit-fucker." I look around:

no one's heard. I toe one of the raviolis, pushing it toward the others. The pile of yellow squares spreads under the table and toward the stove, with bright red sauce between them and small brown chunks of meat. Several options of how to clean up the mess run through my mind: a mop, a broom and a dustpan, paper towels, a sponge and water. But none of these seem right. The vacuum, I decide. I go to get it out of the hall closet. I have to crawl under my mom's coats to get to the back, but I find the vacuum and drag it out by the hose, then go back in for the long tube. I put it all together, then wheel it into the kitchen, plug it in next to the answering machine, and turn it on.

I touch the hose-end to my hand to make sure it's sucking, and it pulls on my skin, so I attach the tube and run it across the floor, headed for the outer raviolis. Schloop, it pulls in the first one. I look down the tube and it's gone. I aim the tube at the other raviolis. Schloop, it pulls in another. Even some of the sauce is getting cleaned up off the floor, and the little pieces of meat disappear as I head for the biggest patches of food. Schloop, schloop the tube sounds as it pulls them in.

"What are you doing?" I hear. My mom runs over to the vacuum and turns it off, kneeling down. It makes a kind-of-wheezing sound, something it's never done before. My mom unplugs the hose and looks inside, then stands and hits the end of the tube against the sink. Nothing happens. "If you broke this vacuum, Adam, you're going to buy a new one," she says.

Rachel watches us from the doorway to her room, thumb in her mouth. She has on her pink nightgown.

My mom hits the hose end against the side of the garbage. One of the raviolis falls out. "Why did you do this to the vacuum," she asks. I back toward the wall. "What made you think you should use the vacuum?"

what happened to everything

I look at my feet and the raviolis. "I don't know."

She closes the space between us in two steps and grabs my face, holds it so I'm looking at her. She has her hand under my chin, her fingers squeezing into my cheeks. "What is wrong with you?" she says, her face close to mine. "What!"

I don't know what to say. My face hurts where she squeezes. I stay still, trying not to do anything. Then she lets me go. She goes to the sink and takes out a roll of paper towels from underneath, wets a handful and gets down on her knees and starts wiping the raviolis into a pile. I want to help, so I kneel down to try and hold my hand out. Instead of letting me help, she lowers her head, wiping food and sauce from under the table. "Leave me alone," she says, so I back away to the other side of the room.

Opposite from where I stand, Rachel starts crying, her thumb still in her mouth, which is now bent around it, her sobs coming freely.

"Shit," my mom says. "Shit." She touches her face, and I can see a tear at the end of her nose. She wipes her wrist across her face, but not before the tear lets go. I see it fall quietly and hit the floor, disappearing into the mess among the red sauce, meat chunks, and raviolis. She puts the paper towels down and sits back against the cabinets with her knees bent in front of her. "What happened to us today?" she says. Her voice is so soft it's like a whisper. When she says this, she hits the back of her head against the cabinets. Rachel cries louder, comes across the room to my mom, who takes her into her arms. "We tried to do everything fun. We went to the pool. We stopped at McDonald's." She hits her head against the cabinet for each "We," hugging Rachel to her chest.

It surprises me when she opens her eyes. "What happened,

Adam?" she says, crying, looking at me with wet eyes, her chin crinkled. She holds her arms out wide, letting go of Rachel, and says, "What happened to everything?" as if to show me she means the whole apartment, or the world.

I am as still as a statue, waiting for my mom to be OK.

"What happened?" she screams, looking right at me. Then, as if I'm supposed to know what she means, or the answer, she says it again, "What happened?"

"I don't know."

"No," she says. "No."

I bend down and start cleaning with the paper towels, but everything I do only moves sauce around, leaves streaks in new lines. The paper towels come apart in my hands and I try to scoop it all up: the sauce, the raviolis, the paper. I get the pile into a clump and lift it to the sink.

"Don't," my mom says, quiet. She puts her hand against my shin. She opens the cabinet under the sink and holds the garbage can out to me. "We don't have a disposal," she says. "We had one at our old house, but not now." When she says "old house" she means when we lived in the Back Bay, with my dad.

I drop the brown mess into the garbage. My mom helps Rachel out of her lap and to standing, then rises herself. Rachel is tuned out, watching us with empty eyes. She walks away into the living room, lays down on the rug. I look up at my mom, wanting to exchange a look that says we both know Rachel's crazy, but that doesn't happen. My mom leads me to the sink and gets the water running. I hold my hands out to her, and she takes them and rubs my hands between hers, soaping them, and then runs both our hands under the water. The water feels warm, exactly like it should be, not too hot or too cold. She rinses the soap off my palms and then the backs of my hands, then rinses her own hands.

She kisses the top of my head.

I look down at the floor, the vacuum cleaner.

"Pick that up," she says, pointing at the hose, and I do. She takes the other end and pulls the hose straight so that we can both look through it at the same time and see each other's eye. "They're not in here," she says. She winks. "I bet they're in here." She opens the vacuum and removes the bag, shakes it around. I hear something hitting the sides. "That's where they got to, most of them anyway." She throws the bag away and takes a new one from under the sink, puts it in. "Take this back to the closet," she says, meaning the vacuum. "OK little man? And then we'll eat some lunch, and we can all take naps, or read, or you can play on the computer."

"Can I put on the radio?"

She nods while she starts taking things out of the refrigerator, and I drag the vacuum back to the closet, new bag and all, go into the living room where the stereo is. It has Thriller on the turntable, but I put on the radio to 103.3 just as "Safety Dance" is starting. I dance around the living room and chop my hands through the air like a robot when the mechanical music starts, and when I come back into the kitchen my mom's got a can open and I can smell the tuna and the mayonnaise, and the bread toasting in the toaster.

I sit down at the table as my mom mixes the ingredients in a bowl. I can hear the spoon hitting the side of the glass and "Safety Dance" playing behind it: "S…s…s…s… A…a…a… a… F…f…f…f… E…e…e…e…"

I close my eyes and imagine that this isn't just a normal playing of the song; I imagine that it's reached Number One on this week's countdown. I know this will happen one day, when everything comes right, and imagine that that's now.

"Safe safe safe safe… Dance dance dance dance…"

Casey Kasem has just run down the top forty songs in the land and reached Number One and it is "Safety Dance" by Men Without Hats. It is The Top Song in The Land, I tell myself, smiling.

I imagine that in our kitchen my mom makes three sandwiches on white bread, with orange juice and potato chips for all three of us. She puts the tray of sandwiches down on the table in front of me, and Rachel comes in from her bedroom without her thumb in her mouth. She is smiling, wearing the pink t-shirt and her tan shorts. Her hair is pulled up into a neat pony tail and she looks pretty. My dad is here and we're back in our old house, the one with the disposal and the nice kitchen, the big wooden deck and the new-model stove. I have my own room, my own TV. I imagine my mom smiling as she sets the plates of sandwiches at our places. Each of us has our own: a sandwich and chips. My father smiles and thanks my mother, touches her on the wrist.

Each sandwich is cut in half on its diagonal. There are pickles. Rachel says thank you to my mother, and I do too.

I hold my eyes closed. I listen to the music.

rebuilding men

My father and I do exercises together at night to get in shape. I am in the sixth grade and my father lives in a Boston suburb called Lexington. He and I are single men who could use some work around our midsections. We build our muscles; my father says we are rebuilding men.

On the thick orange rug in the second-floor hallway, we hook our feet behind each other's ankles and do sit-ups. We do sets of twenty, taking turns—him, then me.

A book dictates our regimen with pictures: seven exercises each night, cardiovascular and stretching, that take us through our whole bodies two and a half times each week. We do push-ups, sets of eight, and then move to calf-raises, on the stairs, each of us holding the banister. Because of my father's bad back, we do extra work on our stomachs: lying flat on our bellies in the hall, face to face, we hold our heads and feet off the ground for an eight-count. My father tells me I'm good at this, but it's no trouble, to me it's flying. On our second rep we hold our arms out in front, stretched straight, our hands almost touching. I imagine the air blowing past, my feet out straight and my hands up high. I hold my breath and imagine I'm Superman. We balance on our stomachs until my father counts to eight, then rest, one cheek on the rug, before going up for another, our arms stretched behind us this time, as far as the hallway will let them. I'm a plane now, an F-14 Tomcat flying with my wings tucked in.

For dinner we eat fish sticks and frozen vegetable medley. My father refuses to use the microwave until we have it tested for radiation—we're only renting the house—so I'm in charge of steaming the vegetables. My other job is to mix mayonnaise and relish to make tartar sauce, and both of us watch my sister to make sure she doesn't get into trouble. She's five.

"We're getting a new tenant," my Dad says, "A girl who's going to move into the third floor apartment and live with us."

"I don't need a baby-sitter," I say.

"I just feel better if someone's around when you get home. Mostly she'll be taking care of Rachel. She'll also have a car."

"You're the only one who can help me with my homework," I say.

"Tammy will be able to help you. She's very smart."

"Tammy?"

"Watch out you don't burn that." He takes the vegetables off the stove.

"But she's not as smart as you are," I say. "You can't promise that."

My dad opens the lid and looks in at our vegetables. "She'll just be here," he says.

• • •

The day Tammy moves in, I have to help her carry her boxes up the stairs. She is manly with a wide face and blond straight hair with bangs like a helmet. She wears blue jeans and her hips are wider than my dad's. There is a guy with her, who says his name is Mike. He carries the heaviest boxes, and jokes with Tammy about their cars, but he does not shake hands with my father. We offer them iced tea made from powder, but they do not drink it. I gulp down two glasses. Tammy laughs and says she thinks I'm cute. She stands with her hands on her hips and laughs. She says we're going to have some fun together, her and her cuties.

"I'm in sixth grade," I tell her. She's still laughing. "I'm no cutie," I say. She tells my father that she'll be sure and watch what she calls me. My sister hugs onto her leg.

• • •

Tammy's bedroom is just above mine. That night in the dark I can hear her rusty bed-springs. I think her and Mike are up there screwing, that this is what I hear. At first it starts out just a creaking sound that comes slow, but it gets quicker. I wonder if my father can hear it, if there's anything he will do, but his room is all the way down the hall. The sound gets faster, metal springs stretching then releasing, as if someone's jumping on the bed up there—like I used to do at our old house when my mom still lived with us—and then all at once it stops. There are a few more noises, but mostly it's quiet. I guess that's how screwing stops.

Mike's car is gone when we're eating breakfast. My dad says Tammy will be there when we get home from school, and that I'm not supposed to give her any lip. I want to tell him about the screwing, but Tammy comes into the kitchen. She's wearing a pink bathrobe and I can see her legs under the edge of it, her thick calves, and when she sits down I get a peek up higher on her thighs.

At school I tell Allen Sherman about the sounds. He thinks it's funny, that the noises a bed can make are worth imitating all morning in class. "Eek-er, eek-er," it sounds like he's saying. Catherine Gill hears him and she asks what we think we're doing. I tell her nothing important is going on.

To the other kids in my class I'm still just a new kid, some guy who moved out to the suburbs when his parents split up, and mostly they don't notice me. The ones that do think I'm weird. But Allen Sherman's my friend and Catherine Gill at least knows my name. She's from England or someplace like that, and she talks funny, but the others seem to like her. She lives behind our house, up the hill, and sometimes she walks by while I'm in the yard. The most she ever says to me is hi, but at least she knows my name.

We're having sex education classes twice a week now, and Mr. Strether lets the girls go out of our classroom to meet with the nurse. When they're gone, he explains to us how the male reproductive aspects of copulation occur and shows us a diagram of the penis to explain what an erection is. He says things like vas deferens and seminal vesicle. Allen Sherman's holding his hands in his lap and has his lips sewn together like he's biting them closed, not breathing, trying to keep from laughing, and I'm not doing much better.

"Boner," he whispers.

We both get thrown out of class.

rebuilding men

• • •

Afternoons I play with Allen Sherman in the yard. We play badminton or hit rocks over the neighbor's houses with the rackets. He's not very good at badminton, but the fact that he can serve makes him better than Rachel, and Tammy won't play badminton for some reason. He shows off sometimes, like he'll dive for ones he doesn't have to, just so he can jump on the ground, and then I'm laughing so hard I usually don't hit it back. He looks funny all stretched out in the air, going after one he could've just hit by stepping sideways, and then he slams to the ground so loud it's even funnier.

Catherine Gill walks by while we're playing. She can see us through the hedge and we see her, but no one's talking. She's just there for a while and I'm hoping Allen won't do anything stupid. I realize I'm wearing the brown sweatpants I wear every weekend—only on the weekends!—and I kind of wish Catherine didn't see me in them, that I was wearing my new parachute pants instead.

"Hi," she says.

"Hi."

"We're playing badminton," Allen Sherman tells her.

"I was just walking home—"

Just at that moment, Tammy yells to ask what we're doing. She can't see us behind the garage. "I'm going to the mall," she yells. "Do you two want to go?"

"No!" I call back, though Allen Sherman's already on his way toward the house. He gives me a look that lets me know he wanted to go. He's been all talk about what new module for Marvel Universe might be in at the Kay Bee.

"What are you up to?" I say to Catherine.

"Let's play badminton," Allen Sherman says, and he hits the birdie up real high and with enough arc on it that it lands on the top of the garage. It bounces once on the roof, then stays up there.

"Oh," I say.

"How're you going to get that down?" Catherine asks.

"We'll climb up there," I say, trying to shrug it off. "Do you want to play?"

"No thanks. I should get home."

"Oh."

"There's only two rackets anyway," Allen Sherman says.

"And you'll have to fetch your shuttlecock."

Allen Sherman starts laughing. "Shuttlecock," I hear him say.

"There are others," I say, but Catherine shakes her head. "That's fine," she says, raising her hand. "I should get home." She looks up the hill toward her house, finger-brushes hair around the back of her ear, and looks down at her foot, then up to the birdie on top of my garage. "I'm having a party," she says. "It's not for a while, but I'll start inviting people soon."

"Oh."

"Excellent then." She waves, and starts walking home. I watch her go until I can't see her any more behind the hedges.

Allen Sherman claps me on the back. "That's one of the parties, my man. You're going to a dancing party."

All year long the cool kids have been having weekend dancing parties that I haven't been invited to. "Okay," I say. "But I can't dance."

"It's like this," he says, holding his hands out straight from his hips, elbows locked into his sides, rocking from one foot to the other. "All you have to do is sway with them. Nothing like what you see people doing on TV. None of that fancy crap." It seems hard to imagine Allen Sherman with a girl actually letting him put his hands on her, but he's still rocking like he knows.

"Where are your hands?"

"On the girls," he says. "Right on their hips."

"Really?"

"Yeah," he says, rocking. Then he stops. "Well, whatever," he says. "Give me ten fingers and I'll climb up to get that birdie."

"I'll go up," I say, so Allen gives me ten fingers and from there I can get a good grip on the gutter, then, stepping on a window, I get one knee up and from there I'm on the roof. I throw the birdie down to Allen and take a good look around the world: up the hill to see if I can still see Catherine, but she's gone; there's a big blue sky all around, just a few white clouds over in the direction of downtown. For a minute, just a few seconds really, I catch myself thinking it's not so bad living in the suburbs and going to this new school, only visiting my mom a few nights a week. Allen Sherman's down on the lawn, looking up at me, my friend. "It's not so bad here," I say. "I'm going to a party!"

"Come down, you knob!"

It's too high to jump from standing, so I sit on the side of the roof and slide my butt over the edge of the gutter, like I've done other times, but this time something breaks and I crash down onto the grass with a big piece of the garage.

"Shit!" Allen says. "Are you okay?"

I stand up and look at the garage. The whole gutter on the back side is off. It's on the ground where I fell, and it doesn't look like something Allen Sherman and I can fix before Tammy gets back, or ever. "Damn," I say.

When my dad comes home I tell him the gutter got knocked off the garage and when he asks me how that happened, I have to explain to him about climbing up to get the birdie. It's late, so we have to take a flashlight outside with us to look, and he shines it along the edge of the roof where the gutter used to be and then he touches the used-to-be-attached part, running his finger along it.

"Well. You broke that one right off." he says. He looks up to where it used to be and lets out a long, rising whistle. "How did you get up there?"

"Allen Sherman gave me a boost up and then I climbed on the shutter."

"You know we're renting this house, Adam. This garage isn't even ours?"

"I'm sorry Dad, I didn't mean it."

"I know," he says. He turns the flashlight off and pats me on the back. "I know, Adam. I'm just looking for some help is all."

"I know, Dad. I'll try."

• • •

My dad and I have a new book that we're doing yoga exercises out of. There's one where we stand facing each other and press our hands together, lean forward until our top halves are parallel to the ground. It's supposed to help our flexibility, which is good for my dad's back.

"How old were you when you went to your first boy-girl party?" I ask between sets.

"I guess I was about your age."

"Were there girls you liked there?"

"I guess," he says. "I guess there must've been one or two I thought were nice-looking."

"When did you kiss one?" I ask. "A girl."

"Older than you."

"What did you like about them?"

My dad gives me a look that lets me know we're supposed to be relaxing between exercises. "I'm not sure I knew then, Adam. I think at your age it's just something you go through." He counts to five and we bend forward. All our other fingers touch at the tips, except for the pinky on my father's right hand. That one won't bend anymore because he cut the tendon when he slammed a knife into our dining room table at the old house, after my mom left.

I know the kind of knife that did it because we still have some of them left in the drawer. Its blade was not sharp or serrated. It wouldn't cut meat; it was made for buttering toast and cutting green beans on your plate. It is all metal, from the handle to the blade and if you hit the table with it like my dad did, it could slip up through your hand and cut your finger.

We stand up again, my father across from me, older and gray, taller than I am, his hands against mine—strong hands, playing the piano strong. "One more set," he says. We are in the upstairs hall and I know that downstairs in our dining room our table has three holes in it. I know that these holes are from when my father stabbed it with the knife. I've put my fingers in them; I know them: the first hole is a deep well, half as wide as a dime. It goes through the veneer and into the wood as deep as the tip of my finger to the nail. The second hole is a shallow gash where the knife slipped as it hit the table and went in at an angle, splintering the wood.

"Down," my father says, and we bend forward. We push against each other's hands for balance. I can feel the little machine on my father's pinky touching the side of my left hand. It has a spring in it and it covers his finger, trying to make it straighten. It feels foamy, like styrofoam, and it just brushes my finger. I look straight down at our feet and the dark orange rug. My father has said that he thinks the carpet in this house is hideous, but since we're only renting he's not going to get involved.

The third hole in the table is only as wide as the knife's blade because that was where the knife met the hard wood that stopped it and pushed the blade up into my father's hand. I can only fit the end of my fingernail into that one.

"Up," he says, and we push against each other until we are standing. Then we drop our hands and take a few good breaths.

• • •

The first weekend the town pool's open, Tammy takes us swimming—Allen Sherman is allowed to come. At the pool, her wet red bathing suit is all nipples and I am all eyes. She sits in the sun and I stand in the shallow end, seeing her nipples. I am hard in the cold water. Rachel keeps swimming around. Tammy's bathing suit is like it's invisible. The water is cold and Allen Sherman says, "It's cool we can see her tits," but I remember Mr. Strether saying they were areolas.

rebuilding men

Allen Sherman stands in the shallow end next to me. When I look at him I can see the head of his penis is stuck up over the waistband of his trunks, against his stomach. "For your viewing pleasure," he says.

"That's nice." He just smiles, stands there, showing me his head. This isn't the first time he's showed me. He knows it's big and that makes him confident about showing it around. I guess he's funny that way.

I swim away, out to the deep end, feeling the water swish on my body and rush past my genitals. I hang on the side in the deep end, watching the girls go off the boards in the diving pool. They have bikinis on, some of them, and it isn't much different than wearing underpants. They would do anything to keep you from seeing their underpants at school, but get them to the pool and you can see their legs clear up to the tops.

Tammy won't swim with us, but after a while she gets up and walks to the diving pool, her feet slapping on the cement. Her butt comes out of her bathing suit a little, but not in a bad way, in a way that's kind of good, like just the sides of the bottom are showing: lines above her thighs. She waits her turn in the high-dive line like the others, then she climbs up the ladder like she's not worried at all, even though it's the highest board she's going off of, and strides to the end, bounces once— her body doing a shake when she hits and her breasts making one simple, gentle bounce—and comes up kicking high into the air, holding her arms out to her sides, rotating until her head points down, and then arms-forward she slices into the pool.

When she gets out I can see her nipples even better.

They're darker from the cold water and the suit clings to them now it's wet, outlining them perfectly. I can see through the suit they're brown and shriveled, like your fingers when you stay in the water for a long time.

Allen Sherman is looking at girls' butts underwater. He's missing the world, I think, and I'm glad to have Tammy. He ducks underwater and swims behind a girl and grabs her. She screams, but he's already swimming in the other direction, weaving in and out of the mothers teaching their babies how to kick.

• • •

The night I'm supposed to go to Catherine's party, I help my dad fold laundry. Rachel is spending the night at my mom's, where I was supposed to go, but because of the party I've stayed with my dad. The sweatshirt I want to wear doesn't go into the dryer because we don't want to shrink it, so it's been drying on a towel all afternoon, and it still feels damp.

We're having pork chops and frozen vegetables again for dinner, something that's become one of my semi-favorites, and Dad still won't let me cook my vegetables in the microwave. "Can I still wear that shirt, even if it's not dry?" I ask.

"It'll dry. But until it does you'll be wearing a wet shirt."

"Right," I say. "That's okay."

He makes a face. "Are you excited?"

"I'm not excited," I say, then, "Why do you think they invited me?"

"Why? I think they probably like you and want you to come and have fun."

"None of them like me, I don't think. I'm sure they don't. They think I'm a total nerd." The vegetables look finished so I drain them and put the pot on the table. My father brings over the pork chops.

"It'll be fun," he says.

Outside I can hear Mike's car pulling into the driveway, spraying gravel against the garage, the horn already honking. "So you think I should go then?"

"I think you should do what you want to, but I think you'll be missing a good opportunity if you stay home."

Tammy comes down wearing a short-cut skirt, not quite a mini. "I'll see you men tomorrow," she says.

"Okay," my dad tells her.

When she sees I'm not wearing my usual weekend sweatpants and T-shirt, she knows something's up. She comes back into the kitchen. "What are you all dressed up for?" she asks.

"Me?"

"He's going to a party tonight," my father says.

"Really?" Tammy looks like she just heard I won a beauty pageant. She's got her hands balled up in the middle of her chest like I'm some kind of sucker darling, and she's almost to the point of cooing. "You're blushing," she almost sings.

"It's a boy-girl party," my dad says. "With dancing."

"Really. Are you going to dance with the ladies tonight, killer?"

"I'll probably dance," I say.

"Sounds good to me," she says. "But don't stay out too late." She winks at my father, as she heads out the door. I can hear Mike revving his engine in the driveway.

"Do you think my shirt's dry yet?"

He cups his hand on my elbow, feeling the sleeve. "It's not bad," he says. "You'll be fine."

My father puts down his knife and fork and shakes his head. "I'm sorry about all the trouble I've caused you by moving us out here," he says.

"Dad, you don't have to—" He holds up his hand.

"I know you were more confident in Boston than you are here, and that you had better friends. You seemed happier there. This year hasn't been the easiest, but I wanted to say I'm proud of how you're adjusting. This party will be fun."

"But it was Mom's fault, wasn't it?" I ask. "Mom was the one who made you sell the house and then we had to move out here, right? It's not your fault. Mom's the one who left!"

He nods. "I know, Adam, but it's not just your mother. Everything was both of us. We made some decisions together." He just looks at me, not smiling. "It can't be blamed on either one of us. It's just something that happened."

"I wish it hadn't."

"I know," he says. "I don't blame you. Sometimes I wish the same thing."

Neither one of us says anything for a while and then my father starts cutting his pork chop. "Eat your food," he says.

I eat a bite of vegetables, some pork chop with applesauce on it. "Mom was the one who wanted to leave, right?"

He goes on eating, then nods. "I'm sorry it's had to affect you like this," he says.

"It's not that bad here," I tell him. "We're doing all right."

rebuilding men

"I know, Adam. I know." He looks at his watch and acts surprised. "You should get up there," he says. "It's almost a quarter past eight."

"Okay. Okay." I run upstairs to try and gel my hair and when I come down my father tells me I look good, that I'm going to have fun. I give him the biggest hug I can give him, and then I'm out the door.

Outside the sky is red where the sun's setting and clear blue in front of me, starting to darken. It's the hottest night we've had in a while, and I hope my sweatshirt will keep me cool. The hill up to Catherine's is too steep to ride, so I walk my bike beside me. At the top I start pedaling. The air blows past as I ride, cooling me and drying my shirt. I like the way it feels.

At Catherine's, I lock my bike to the street sign on her corner. I brush my hands off, make sure I'm not sweaty. Tonight I'm supposed to be a dancer, some kind of ladies' man who knows how to slow dance and hold girls' waists. "Fa, la la, la la," I say, testing my voice. As I walk through the house I can hear music playing in the back, and when I get to the deck, I see most of the kids from my class—the cool kids: Paul Napolitano and Tony Armaresco and Mark Sanders are all there, Zach Taylor and Amy Tasker, Alison Olesky, Katie Martilla, Ethan Zahn and even the Zelli sisters! The nerdiest kid here is Greg Lawson, but he's got leukemia or something, and that means everyone has to be nice to him, like there's a rule he has to be included.

Allen Sherman comes over and claps me on the back. "Relax, my man. We're here to have fun. Talk to some ladies." He walks off, headed for the Zellis. After a little while Mark Sanders takes Tina Zelli out into the middle of the deck and the two of them start rocking back and forth with his hands on her hips and hers on his shoulders. His arms aren't straight, but he's not hugging her either. They're just swaying from one foot to the other with his hands on her hips! By the time the first song's over, Tony Arm, Paul Nap, and Zach Taylor have girls and they're dancing too. Tony Arm is dancing with Catherine Gill!

By the second song, all the girls are dancing and Greg Lawson and I are the last two boys on the side. When I see Stacy Zimmerman standing by the sodas, I go over and ask if she wants to dance. It's gotten so it's more embarrassing to be not dancing than it is to try and dance, is the best that I can understand how I pull this off. Stacy must be thinking the same, because she says yes and we move out onto the edge of the group.

I put my hands on her hips and Stacy's hands come up on my shoulders. I can feel her jeans and where her belt is, and even, just a little, with my first fingers, where her skin is above her belt, where her body sticks out over her jeans. Her shirt is thin, some kind of silky material, and her skin feels soft and smooth through it.

When her hands move on my shoulders I wonder if she's uncomfortable because I'm taller than her, if I should let her move her hands down onto my arms. I realize I'm hard and I don't want to bump up against her or for her to brush me and find out, so I turn my hips away and use my arms to hold some space between us. We keep dancing. It's just another slow song off the radio, something I can barely hear, but it doesn't matter because all I have to do is sway with Stacy.

rebuilding men

I want to say something cool but I have no idea what it should be. Telling her she has big boobs seems entirely incorrect. "Hi," I say.

"This is a nice house," Stacy says.

"Nice deck."

"Yeah."

I feel like I should still say something, so I ask if she likes the music. She says she does but she also likes some of the fast stuff on the radio, too. She lists a couple of bands. "Yeah," I say. "I like them."

After the song ends everyone moves to someone near them who has no partner. I dance with Amy Tasker and Katie Martilla, girls I wouldn't even have thought of asking to dance with me, and they're actually nice about it. None of them bumps into me, either, so I don't think they realize I'm hard. I seem to be doing okay. After a few songs, I'm standing in front of Catherine Gill when the music starts and we're dancing.

She's wearing a dress. I don't know where her hips are, exactly, but I put my hands where I think they are and then I slide down until I feel them, careful not to be gropey. My hands are sweaty, but I don't think she'll be able to feel it, and I wonder if my shirt is still damp, but she doesn't say anything. "I like your party," I say.

"My mom just had this deck added on," she says, and right then, right when she says this, someone bumps into her from behind and she knocks into me, bumps full on into my wood.

"Sorry," she says. "I—"

"I'm sorry," I say. "I'm sorry about the badminton."

"The what?"

I don't know what else I can say or what I should do. If one of us says "shuttlecock," I think I'll die.

"Oh," she says, "Let's just dance," she says, and I do that, I just dance with her, listening to the music—a slow song I don't know the name of—and somehow I keep my mouth closed.

All the cool kids in my class are on that porch, dancing, and there isn't much talking, which seems okay. The night is warm, and my shirt is dry. I see them all around me; I'm dancing with Catherine Gill and everyone else is there. There's a light on Catherine's face that doesn't seem to be on any of the others' and her smile is brighter than anyone else's. I hold my hands on her tightly, and sway with her slowly, as slowly as we can, until the song is entirely over.

Catherine slides away, smiling, and after that I take a break. Allen Sherman's by the chips and carrot sticks. "Pretty good party," he says.

"Yeah." I'm afraid he'll accuse me of liking Catherine Gill, but he goes off to dance with Stacy Zimmerman.

Pretty soon someone says it's the last song, and then before I know it, the party starts winding down. I go over to Catherine to thank her, and I tell her I'm glad I came. "Thank you," she says. "It was nice of you to be here."

I sneak away from the others and take my bike, go the wrong direction for a block so I don't have to ride past all the mothers picking people up, then cross back over to my street and head home. Catherine's smile looked prettier than ever when she said goodbye to me, the air's blowing past and it's like the bike is going on its own; I'm hardly pedaling. I hold my hands up off the handlebars for one second, two, before clapping them back down. Something about the whole night, the party, my shirt, dancing with Catherine seems funny; I start laughing. "It's all okay," I say out loud, to no one. The wind's rushing past me and I almost feel like I'm flying—this is how I should've dried my shirt, I realize.

I start pedaling faster when I see the hill coming. I want to ride it as fast as I can. Even if there's a big street at the bottom, with cars, I feel like I can fly down the hill and there won't be anyone in my way. I want to ride it fast this one time, can feel there won't be cars coming. Everything will be fine. I'm going to ride the hill. I pedal harder to get there going as fast as I can, and then at the top I stand on the pedals, leaning over the handle bars, feeling the wind on my face. The air's blowing faster than ever, the ground beneath my feet is a blur of dark concrete, the circle of light from the streetlight flashing past beneath me. Though the big street's coming, I don't slow down. I don't even look up. I watch the pavement flying past beneath me. I'm going like lightning. At the bottom I'm going faster than I ever have. The world is silence and stillness.

All around I can see the houses I've always seen, only now I feel like I know them, understand all of what's going on inside, who these people are and why they should feel the way they do, and who we are and where we fit and where we're going. I see the trees on our neighbors' lawns, the grass freshly groomed, and the squared-off fine hedges lining the foundation of their homes. Behind the lights in the windows they are happy and I'm looking toward our house, trying to get a sense of how our windows look from the outside, when I hear the first horn. The first screech of brakes.

Then I see the truck.

I hear his screeching brakes and the horn but he's right on top of me and I pull my brakes as hard as I can, and skid on the ground, falling. My leg's caught underneath, under my bike, and I slide on it; the truck's brakes make a sound like an eagle screaming but it's stopping—it stops before it hits me. When everything resumes, my bike is still between my legs with the truck's lights blaring right at me.

The driver opens his door and gets out, runs around to the front where I am. "You all right, kid?" I can see his dark blue pants in the headlights. He is a big man.

"I think so," I say.

He picks me up under the armpits and sets me down on my feet. "Let me see you," he says. My leg hurts to stand on and my hands sting. My elbow hurts. The man bends down, puts his face in front of mine, his eyes glaring. "Do you know you could have killed yourself!" he says. "I didn't see you. I could've hit you! Do you realize that?"

I sit down, trying not to cry. I can see the blood on my hands.

"Do you see this?" the man says, pointing at his truck. "This is a truck! Do you understand what that means? Let me show you something!" He bends down then, and holding his hair apart with both hands, shows me his scalp. I see a line across his head where the brown hair doesn't grow. A white line. "Do you know how I got this?" he says. "Just like that," he says, pointing to the truck. "Riding my bike when I was young and dumb as you. Not looking, no helmet, just like you. You see that scar? Twenty-five stitches it took. And I was lucky!"

I can't help it anymore; I start to cry.

He shows me his scalp again. "I almost just killed you, kid."

"I'm sorry."

"I know," the man says, hands on his hips. He shakes his head.

"Can you stand?" he asks. I nod and he helps me up. He lets go of me, picks up my bike. "Where do you live?"

"Over there," I lie, pointing behind some houses down the street. "I'm okay," I tell the man. "I can walk home."

"You were lucky," the man says, shaking his head. "You got to be more careful next time. This is a hell of a thing this life." He pulls my face up by my chin so that I'm looking into his eyes. "You know that?" he says, spreading his other arm to gesture as far as he can reach. "This is it, kid. You want to lose this?" I shake my head, wiping the tears off my cheeks. "I didn't think so." He puts my bike on the sidewalk, then walks around to the front of his truck, spits a long, dark stream on the road, and gets in.

My bike's handle-grip is scraped off on its side, the side that I fell. It's a white grip that had ridges full-around it, but now they're scraped so that the plastic's flat and I can see the metal underneath. The handle bar seems turned in a little, curved more than it should be, like my father's finger.

When I push it, the front tire wobbles, but the bike still rolls. I walk it back up the hill, to the garage, and lay it on the grass behind my house. I don't want to cry, but I am, and then, walking up the porch steps in the dark, I see the kitchen light still on, and my dad at the table. I stand up straight and wipe my face with my sleeve.

When I go in, he looks up and I can see his face go from good to bad. He gets up and comes over. "What happened to you?" he says.

"I fell."

He holds my thigh steady and touches my knee. "Does this hurt?" He brings me to the sink and holds my hands under the cold running water. I can see bits of white skin wiggling on my palms. He rubs my back. "Do you feel okay?" he says this, getting the paper towels.

"I'm sorry," I say, trying not to cry.

My dad hugs me, holding my head against his chest.

"I'm sorry, Dad. I didn't mean for this to happen."

"It's okay, Adam," he says. "I know you didn't. Of course you didn't." He holds me until I stop crying, then puts my hands back under the cold water. They're stinging, tingly with the cold. "How was your party?" he asks. I nod and move my hands out of the water to let him wet a paper towel. He kneels down and rolls up my pants leg, touches the scrape gently. "Run some cold water on that elbow."

I roll up my sleeve and hold my arm under the cold. It shocks at first, and I see blood running down the drain. "I danced, Dad."

"I'm glad for that, Adam."

For some reason I laugh. "It was fun, Dad. The people were nice. Even the girls." I watch the water take the dirt away from my elbow. It comes clean and I can see the fresh white of the scrape.

That's when Tammy walks in; she's standing at the back door, with Mike. I stand up straight and wipe my face off with the backs of my hands. "What happened to you?" she asks, rushing over.

"He fell."

"It's just a scrape," I say.

rebuilding men

"A couple scrapes!" She takes my hands in hers, holds my palms up to see. "Oh, Adam," she says.

"I fell off my bike."

Very lightly, she kisses my left palm and then my right.

"He went to the party," my dad says. "Even danced with girls!"

Tammy's face brightens. "You danced?" She makes a sweep around the kitchen as if she's waltzing, and finishes with a spin and a curtsey. "With girls?"

"Not like that," I say. I can't help laughing.

"Of course not big guy." She touches my chin. "But you danced."

My dad stands up. He pats my shoulder and holds my elbow up to take a look.

"And were the ladies all very crazy about you?" Tammy asks. "Because they will be." She steps closer, almost as if we're dancing, and she touches her finger to the end of my nose. Then she kisses me, right on the side of my face. Mike laughs.

"Let's head up, Tam."

"Okay," she says. "Night, Tiger." She winks and follows Mike upstairs.

"We should get you up to bed," my dad says, closing the door behind them. He puts his arm around my shoulders and leads me into the dining room. "I'm glad you had a good time," he says.

I'm still thinking about Tammy's kiss as we limp across the rug. I try not to look at the holes in the table, but I see them, all three. I know the table's worse than my bike, but I think of the plastic grip and the bent handlebars. "Can you tell me if my bike's okay, Dad? The handlebar's bent a little, but I think it'll ride." I try to turn back toward the kitchen. "Come see it."

"You'll show me tomorrow, Adam."

"I want to show you now, Dad. My bike's okay, I think, but we should see." I look at my palms, the red still tender.

"In the morning," he says. He rubs the back of my head, squeezes my neck. "It's late," he says, and turns me back toward the stairs.

We move into the front hall together, my dad's hand under my arm, and when I see the staircase, I remember we forgot to do our exercises. When I tell my dad he just says, "You've had enough excitement for today, pal. Maybe we should take a few days off to let you heal." He pats my back. "We have to get you better."

"We can do the other ones," I say. "Even if my leg hurts and my hands, we can still work on our midsections."

"We'll see," he says.

"I'll be fine," I tell him, and I think I will be fine: I danced with Catherine Gill at a real party, my bike will ride, and Tammy kissed my face. Everything is fine.

"Come on now, Adam," he says. "Up to bed." He points me toward the stairs, holding my arm so I can hop up without bending my knee.

I don't want my dad to start missing workouts, though, or for his back to get soft, so I squeeze him around his middle with both arms. I tell him, "We'll do our sit-ups, Dad. Tomorrow morning. We'll rebuild our backs into iron."

white

They called me wigger and one time this old bag bitch told me, "Keep running with the monkeys and you'll end up back in the jungle with that black girl, swinging from a vine."

But before any of that happened, Dub was the one who first put me on. He brought me down to the courts behind his projects knowing the others wouldn't like him bringing a whitey, but ready to start shit with anyone who said boo. Still, they were like, "Who this white nigger?" and "You trying to bring Larry Bird up in here?"

"This ain't no Indiana," they said, and I got beat. Down low on the blocks and outside the paint, I got used on defense, and they beat my shot like they saw it that morning. Even though I was taller, they were all over me. One kid blocked my shot so bad he hit it twice off the backboard before he came down. That got everyone on the side all up, yelling, "Oooh Bob Cousy! Take that shit back to the farm!" and "Yo, jump white baby! You got to get up to get off in this mother!"

By the time we lost I didn't want to stay. I just tried to

disappear next to Dub, but he brought me off to the side and said, "You got to throw fakes in there, son. Either fake and then go up or kick that shit out. Motherfuckers beating your shit like this was Thanksgiving."

"Right," I said. "Listen, I think I'm going to just be out."

"Nah, yo. You can't go out like that. Stay one more."

I kept my hands down then, not calling for the ball, and went to the boards instead of posting. If I caught enough rebounds and passed them out that start-the-block-party shit couldn't happen, I figured. Our second game, the kids on the side almost stopped yelling white boy.

But this one kid couldn't take it. He wanted to play and we won so I was, and he couldn't take it. He kept asking how could they let a white kid up in there and how could I be on the court if he wasn't. Then he tried to come at me, but Dub caught him by the head and threw him down. He came up throwing punches, but Dub was just too big. All you could see was his top half over that kid's back, Dub's face like he was crazy and his arms pumping down on the kid like pistons. I'd never seen anyone fight like that, not that wild. Dub dropped one punch on him from high up, like a rainbow jumper. It fell hard, then the kid stood still for a second and he wobbled and fell back on his ass like he'd come in half. It was like something you'd dream about, and Dub did it. He landed that punch then started kicking, but the others broke it up.

• • •

Dub could fight. Mornings we stayed at my mom's, he'd do sit-ups and push-ups until he sweat and then he'd run for a little while, throwing punches like the boxers he saw on TV, ducking left and right. I watched him sometimes and thought about it a little when I was alone. I even tried to find my own routine of exercises to start each day with, but it wasn't me. I just played basketball, that was all I wanted.

My parents were split up and my father had just moved to another different town in the suburbs, a place called Newton, but my mom still lived in Cambridge. I was thirteen, living with her to avoid being where I didn't know anybody, and spending long hours on the courts, fighting through games that were anything but.

There was another kid, Drew, who hung out with us sometimes, who wasn't black, but his mom was, so he had half-half status, which basically meant he didn't fit in on either side. Some people called him a halfie and some said he was mulatto, but none of the girls would talk to him because he had freckles and red hair. People used to call him Dennis Johnson—the ugliest player on the Celtics—because DJ had freckles too, and Drew had to fight to get past it, but eventually they eased up because his handle was nice and he could see passes that no one else could.

When Drew and Dub came over, they used to go rounds of punches, hitting each other in the stomach to see who'd give first. They both took their shirts off and warmed up by hitting themselves. Drew was tighter around the middle and he could make his stomach look like he had rocks under his skin. He had muscles on his sides, too, that wrapped around from his back. He was cut. Dub wasn't cut, but he was thick, and you knew the muscles were still there, just under some skin. He had fat, but he could take the shots.

When they started, Drew always went first because he'd lost the last time. They'd go at it until they punched hard enough to knock each others' winds out and, finally, one of them—Drew mostly—would give. Then they'd hit each other in the arms and laugh, and I'd get in on it, and we'd go play ball. The one time I went in with them from the start, tried the game, they both make jokes about how they needed sunglasses to see when I took my shirt off. But I held still and pushed out my stomach until my own set of rocks showed. They were smaller, but I took a few good punches before I quit.

I showed the bruises to Jeanna Thomas at a party afterwards, and she liked them. We went in the room to play seven minutes, and she let me kiss her. I got my hand up under her shirt too, but that was all. This other time we went beyond that when the three of us had three girls in a room with the lights off. I was trying to get my finger inside Jeanna's underpants through her zipper, digging until the space between my knuckles hurt and only feeling the front of her panties, but when the lights came on Dub had Paloma Perez's skirt up over her waist and he was on top of her. Even then Paloma had the body of a woman; she was dating guys from the high school, but Dub had something that made her crazy for his 8th-grade ass.

• • •

Dub had a sister they called Tish. Her real name was Tanisha, but that didn't matter. Everyone called her Tish. Even though she was only going into 7th grade that summer, she was into it all already, and people would say she fucked if they knew Dub wasn't around to hear it. She'd come find us to ask Dub for money, then they'd get in a fight and she'd start punching at him, and he'd have to hold her down until she got calm. Like it ran in the family, she could fight too.

white

Sometimes, like one night we were riding the bus to my mom's house, Tish used to hang with us and it wasn't that bad. She could be cool when she wanted. That time we were just cooling out after some games, Dub and I, going back to my mom's, and she was there. We used to sit in the back of the bus, where the big blue hump was under the benches. Dub would sing to make his voice stutter from the shaking of the big wheel. He did things like that a lot in public, mostly to piss people off, always looking to start something after ball, when he was crazy from the games and the heat.

But the only other people on the bus were some guys coming back from summer school and a few old people with beards—Grandmothers and Grandfathers—heading back to the home on Putnam. Dub let his voice out and held it, jiggling on the hump. Sometimes it worked, but that day there was no one interested, and if anyone did anything it just a couple of old people giving him a look like, I'm too tired to even hear you, kid. But one old bag lady was looking at me. She looked mad, like I stole something and she meant to break me in about it, so I made sure not to look at her. I knew I was dirty from playing, red and sweaty, but I still couldn't see what was wrong. Then she peeled her lips back and showed me her teeth. She had a goatee with white whiskers and a mustache that wasn't blond. She must've been one of the wild ones who lived in the brick building on Linnean, I guessed, and I hoped she wouldn't want anything, that she was just ugly.

The floor of that bus had little black ridges, with white flecks in the rubber. I looked down and thought back on the games from that day, the ones we'd won and the spots on the block where I got it and what I did with it. I was learning to make moves and I was hitting shots now, starting to go up strong and sometimes clapping the board with both hands.

My arm was next to Tish's shoulder. It wasn't that either of us were moving, but the bus was, some, and it moved us so that our arms were rubbing. Tish leaned forward, elbowing her knees, and started rubbing her legs. She got some lotion out of her bag and rubbed it into her hands and then on her calves. She had socks on, and sneakers, but above that she had long thin legs that she kneaded the lotion into. Dub took the bottle and squeezed some on his arms. He told her she would still be ashy, no matter how much lotion she had, and she told him to fuck off.

Then the old lady moved toward me. She stood above me, stinking, ringing the bell for her stop. She made a face like I didn't have any business in the world being there, and said, "You running with these monkeys now? Going back to the jungle to marry this one and learn how they swing from the vines?"

I was like, What? But Dub got up fast, and told her he'd put his foot up her ass. Then the bus stopped and she was climbing out. She had her hand on the railing and held both her bags in the other. When she was gone, all the old people and the summer school kids were looking right at me. Dub's feet and the others' were all pointed my way, too, and I watched Dub's rocking on the ridges when the bus started up. It got real quiet in the back, and no one said anything until Dub asked what the fuck they were all looking at. They were trying not to, but I could tell people were staring.

"What the fuck you want?" Dub said. Then a couple of

construction workers in big workboots—I don't know where they'd come from—told Dub he shouldn't have talked to that woman that way and that he should get off the bus, now. They rang the buzzer and stood over us with their arms folded until Dub and Tish got off. We were somewhere between Central Square and Harvard, where there were just brick buildings, but I got off too. The bus drove off and Dub said, "Fuck it, go back to your white bullshit."

"Fuck," I said. "I didn't make that happen."

"Shit," Dub said. He shook his head, laughed, and then spit. He told me he was taking Tish home and that I should go back to my mom's.

"No," I said, but he took Tish across the street to wait for the bus back their way. The next one uptown was coming, and I got on because I didn't know what else to do, watching them wait while I found my seat. I saw Tish move to wave, but Dub held her wrist down. He wouldn't look my way.

•   •   •

After that I started staying out at my dad's house in Newton for a while, playing at the J.C.C. or shooting around in the driveway. The games at the J.C.C. were easy compared to Dub's complex. The other white kids tried to play defense, but if you could throw a fake you could do whatever you wanted. Plus, they played soft: you could bump into them and push your way toward the basket and they'd call fouls. They passed me the ball when they had it, but they'd make stupid passes other times and I'd be running back on defense, swearing at them. When I got it, I made my shots, which was cool for a while but then little guys kept running at me whenever I touched it, and I'd get tired from holding them off. Either way my shots dried up, then the games were less fun. The games at Dub's stuck in my head though: how kids there played into the night until you couldn't see the ball. I missed winning those games and the feeling of hating the people who beat me when I didn't.

Most afternoons, I shot baskets in my dad's driveway. He had a hoop on the garage, but the driveway was so steep you had to shoot from ten feet back for the basket to be at the right height. If you shot from anywhere else it just messed up your shot, but from up close it was low enough that I could dunk it like Jordan. Or sort of. I'd work on trying reverses off two feet, catching it off the board and one-handing it back in, but mostly I shot my ten-footers. I'd shoot a few and then take it in, try some double-pump windmill, then shoot the freethrows from ten.

One time these three skinheads walked by. Only two of them had shaved heads, and the other had long hair like a hippy. He wore a confederate flag shirt, though. None of them cared.

"You play basketball?" one said.

I took a shot and one of them caught the ball—the littlest one, with a shaved head and high, black boots. "You play basketball and that's why you have to hang with the niggers?" he said. He held the ball. "Is that right?"

"I don't have to do anything," I said. "I play basketball. I have friends."

"Fuck you don't." The big one stepped toward me. He was about two arms from where I stood but his hands were still down by his sides, deciding to be fists or not.

"You want to play with us?" the hippy asked.

"No."

"Because you want to play with the niggers," the little skinhead said—the one still holding my ball. He held the ball out toward me. "You want this?" he said.

He came at me and tried to hit me with the ball but I caught his arms and swung my elbow into his chin like I did in games sometimes, by accident. I heard the smack and the side of his face give, and that was when the big one hit me from behind and knocked me down on the grass. The little one kicked me once, but the big one just stood there holding his fists. My ball rolled down the drive and into the street.

"See what you done?" the big one said. "You lost your ball now." He lurched his shoulders at me and then laughed when I flinched, hocked a greener on the lawn, and said, "You stick to your own, wigger."

• • •

After that I stayed in the house and watched TV. The J.C.C. games were only at night, so I had nothing to do but watch reruns and the old cartoons. I called Dub and we'd talk for a little while, but he never said to come back and I didn't ask. One time he told me about a few of the games, but mostly we'd get quiet and one of us would go.

One time my mom called on the phone. "It's a beautiful day out there," she said. "What are you doing inside? Don't you realize how much I'd give to be outside? You should get out there."

She always talked fast when we were on the phone. "Unh-huh," I said. What's Happening? was just starting.

"Go outside," she said. "You can't sit in front of that TV all day. Why don't you go over and play basketball with Shawn?"

In the opening for What's Happening? three black guys walked down a street in their neighborhood, bouncing a ball. They looked like they were all friends, like they grew up together and, even though one was fat and one was a nerd, they all took turns dribbling, passing each other the ball.

"Honey," she said. "Listen. Do me a favor and go play basketball with Shawn. Come back here and stay over for a night or two. You always seem so much happier when Shawn is around."

I felt bad watching TV after that. The sun was white coming in through the window, and it would be hot out, as well as bright—it was cool and sleepy inside—but I got up and put my shoes on and went out to the front yard. I stretched like I was going to play, like they'd showed us how to do at the J.C.C., and then I got up and walked to where I could catch the train in to Cambridge.

On the green line train I sat in the back. No one looked at me or said anything about what I was or wasn't supposed to be. I was just a kid in dirty shorts and basketball shoes who didn't have any better place to be. A couple of younger kids got on at Brookline Village. They didn't look at me but I gave them the hard stare like I was going to say something. When they saw it, they looked at their shoes and I felt good for a few minutes, until I got to Park Street and people were rushing around in a hurry, and I just shuffled down the stairs to the Red Line.

When I got to Dub's, it was the same as ever: the games looked good. A couple of the kids recognized me and one of them said he didn't have five, that I could play on his team. Tish was there, sitting on the side, probably waiting to ask for money. She didn't see me right off, but when she did she said, "Where you been at?"

white

I tried to act like lacing up my sneakers was the biggest thing in the world to me, like I couldn't hear her, but I was watching her legs so I saw it coming when she kicked me. "I asked where you been at," she said. "We thought you was living with that old white bitch, trying to make up for being a nigger."

"I been around."

Tish pointed to her brother. "Dub here," she said. He fought some guy off under the basket, trying to get position for a rebound, but then someone threw up a fifteen-foot runner and it bounced long to some little guy on the other team.

Tish sat down with both her elbows on her knees and her arms crossed over. Her skin was dry and I could see the white her brother called ashy, but I could also see how thin she was and the muscles in her shoulders. I could see down the armhole of her tank top a little and the white of her bra, just a bit of the shape it held. She had a scar under her arm that looked like a burn from a quarter, like a crescent half-moon.

"You want some gum," she asked. She took it out of her bag and held a stick toward me.

"I like this kind," I said. "But the flavor only lasts about a minute."

"It's better than what you got," she said.

I unwrapped the gum and put it in my mouth. The flavor was there, how it always started out: sweet, like some fruit that grows somewhere you can't imagine. Tish added another piece to what she was chewing. "It tastes good to me," she said.

In the game, a kid tried to dribble along the baseline, but his shot got blocked and when it did the ball came out to Dub, and he put up his soft jumper.

Tish took my hand, and said, "You want to see something?" I pulled my hand away, but when she got up I followed her. She went down an alley between two buildings, then into an empty hallway through a broken-out window. I stopped. "Come on," she said. She led me down the hallway into a room that looked like a den, a place where people might live, or probably smoked crack in. We were the only ones there. I saw an old couch with some blankets, smoke stains on the walls, and glass vials smashed into the floor. The place looked like it'd caught on fire a long time ago and had only partly been saved from burning.

Tish walked along the wall until she got to the doorway, where I was, then she took my hand and led me inside. I could smell something like a mix of smoke and water, like the place would never come dry. She stood in front of me, up close, almost as tall as I was, and smiling. She could have bitten my face or licked my eye if she wanted, but what she did was take my hand and lay it across her thigh. She put her hand over mine and wrapped my fingers around her leg. It felt soft. "You like this?" she asked. "I seen you looking." She moved my hand by the wrist and I could feel how smooth her leg was, like she'd just rubbed in her lotion. Her skin was deep brown but her shorts showed the line where she got lighter. She must have seen where I looked because the next thing she did was bring my hand right up there. The bottom of her shorts brushed my thumb, her skin softer here, and I felt the lightest part with the tips of my fingers, slipping them under the fabric.

"Hold up," she said, and I pulled my hand away, but didn't move. I took her elbow. Her arm was soft, too. Then Tish took her shorts down and she lay on the couch. My mouth was like it didn't exist then, like my voice had gone. I heard air blowing through the window that was louder than I could have imagined speaking. She slid back and I couldn't believe what I saw and didn't know what to do with it, but I kneeled down in front of her and put my fingers on the coffee-ice-cream-colored part of her leg where I'd been touching.

"You want this?" she said.

I wanted it so much I didn't know what to do. Between her legs I saw her everything and I had no idea. There was nothing I wanted more and nothing I was less prepared for. She put her hand down my shorts and squeezed me so tight I closed my eyes.

"Oh," I said. "Shit." I touched her where her hair was and it was softer than I could have imagined. She pushed my hand down to where it was wet and she had her hand on me and that was more than I could take.

"Fuck!" she said. She let go when she felt me coming. "Fuck."

"Fuck," I said. I rolled onto my side and pushed up onto the couch next to her. "Shit."

"What the fuck is wrong with you?"

I leaned back into the couch with my hands on my pants. It was the best I'd ever felt.

"Go play basketball," she said. "Take your dumb ass and go play basketball and don't never come speak to me. Because ball is all you good for. Barely." She pushed me back into the couch and stood up, pulled her shorts up in my face and walked out.

I just sat there. That wet smell was still in the air, but something else was too: part of Tish's lotion and part of us. It was cool inside, like a basement. The couch had some brown spots on it, and I saw some white powder pushed in around one of the buttons, but parts of it were clean too, with yellow and brown stripes. I wiped my hands on the pillows and picked up a little baggie with green trees printed on it. Something inside me felt like I'd done something very wrong, but part of me felt good, too. I kicked a glass vial across the floor, and heard it bounce off the wall.

After a while, I went into the hall and out the window. When I found my way back to the courts, Dub was on the side next to Tish. She was looking away. Dub had his elbows leaned onto his knees, dripping sweat in a puddle.

"What up?" I said. Dub looked up at me, tired from the game, and nodded. Then he looked at me full on, like he knew Tish had just done something wrong and I was a part of it. That, or she'd told him and he was just starting to believe it. "You got next?" I asked.

"What up, man," he said. Then he shook his head and spat. He turned around and looked at one of the other guys there, someone I'd never seen. "You believe this motherfucker?" he said.

The other kid shook his head.

"After everything I did for this motherfucker," he said. Then, like he wasn't tired anymore, Dub stood up. "You got next," he said, pointing at my chest.

"Cool," I said. "Who's our five?"

"No," he said. "Just you." He hit his stomach with his right hand. "You got next this," he said, pointing at me and then at his chest.

Tish watched us. When she saw me looking, she shook her head and waved the back of her hand at me like go away. Then she looked the other direction.

white

"Put your hands up," Dub said. He stepped closer to where I was. "You want your shirt on, or off?"

I kept my shirt on and I tried my best that day, but I was just a confused little white boy taking his best shot at a tough black kid, and then going down from the first real punch I ever took. And when I hit the asphalt there was blood on my hands. The others pulled Dub off me after he only kicked me a couple times.

Don Flamenco's finest round

Drew looked me up and down. He said, "Tell me I can't rip your head off."

I didn't say anything. He made fists and opened his hands. His head only came to my chin, but he had a thin brown mustache across his upper lip. I could see the muscles of his shoulders flexing through his T-shirt and the tension in his forearms as he gripped the air. He walked the sidewalk, pacing like he didn't know what to do next.

The others, Dub and Jerrod, they watched. They'd put me up to calling Drew that morning to accuse him of stealing the five dollars off my sister's bureau, saw a fight was necessary, told me that I needed to get my respect. "You got to throw blows if he's stealing from your household," they said. So I'd called him, told him to come over.

This was all in the summer after night grade, a full year after I first started hanging out with Dub. I'd seen the kids in Newton, my new school, were suburban dickheads. They didn't get me and I didn't want any part of them. My only option was

Don Flamenco's finest round

Dub and the others by his projects, the black kids who could play ball like crazy, called me white nigger and Larry Bird when I came down, fought as a part of their lives. This was closer to where I fit in than anything else.

The heat was still full on then, like the city was an oven that someone had left set to Clean for too long. You sweat no matter what you did. Now basketball took up less of our time, fighting took up more. But usually it was the others that fought, and I just watched.

Around us people walked Mass. Ave. like any other weekday. I could see the line inside Dunkin' Donuts, people waiting to order. A few newspaper machines were lined up along the curb. Dub and Jerrod circled Drew and me, cheering us.

"Tell him," Dub said. Jerrod hooted and pumped his fist.

"Tell me I can't rip your head off."

I looked at my own hands: white like Drew's, not black like Dub's or coffee-colored like Jerrod's, but thin. Not fists. Drew's forehead wrinkled. I knew he fought, that he took kung-fu classes with Jerrod, lifted weights in his room at night.

"You can't rip my head off," I said.

"What?"

"Ooh," the others droned in, trying to stoke it.

Drew and Dub and me, we had gone to school together in seventh and eighth grade. But he had stolen from me, a thing I suspected of Dub, and something I'd caught Jerrod at once, but now I had to fight Drew. It was something I had to do, they said.

"You can't rip my head off," I said.

And with that I let go: I'd known it would happen, that I

had to go through with it. I'd even resigned myself to this fact, but I didn't let go until I said this. And from that moment I knew it was on. Drew lunged at my waist. I was trying to get my hands up as he grabbed at my arms; he seemed like he was trying to pull my head down, and I pushed him off, into the panel glass of the Dunkin' Donuts. He caught me again, held me against the glass, trying for a hold. People inside beat on the window. Drew locked his arm around my head, and I could hear people yelling, "Take it away. Go on, take that somewheres else. This ain't a good place for yous to be fighting."

"Move down, move down," the others yelled as they pushed Drew and me away from the Dunkin' Donuts. The headlock came off, and I could see ladies on the sidewalk staring. An old man with a white T-shirt and a beer belly shook his head and waved his finger.

Drew's face looked wild with anger. A bead of sweat rolled down his temple.

"Yo, around the corner," Dub said. "Mass. Ave's too busy."

"Yeah," Jerrod said. "Yeah."

The four of us walked around the corner to a side street with less traffic. We stood in the middle of the pavement, Dub and Jerrod leaning on cars. Drew still looked mad, and my heart was going wild.

"What you want now?" Drew said.

I rushed at him and pushed him backward into a car. I could hear the others cheering. "Fuck him up," Dub said.

Then Drew turned it and threw me against the car. He tried to grab for my head again, and I fought him off, trying to hold his wrists, but he pushed me back, and we landed on the hood with me bent over backward. Somehow I moved him to my side and we both rolled down the hood and onto the pavement. He landed on top again and held my arms on either side of my shoulders. I did my best to keep my legs moving, just flailing, trying to kick him in the back. "Stop it," he said. He moved up so his knees were on my elbows. He was farther from my legs now, and I couldn't kick him. I kept trying. He slapped me in the face; I knew he could punch me if he wanted, but for some reason he wasn't. "Stop it," he said, but I didn't stop. I kept kicking at him and then, stretching as far as I could, I managed to get my body partly up from under him and, catching my feet under his arms, I threw him off me, into the car.

"Oh, shit," the others called.

"The fuck was that?"

I looked up and saw Drew as surprised as I was, slumped against the front tire. For a moment, I felt good, like I had done something. But then he got up faster than I did, knocked me down, and he was on top again. He hit me in my ribs and I tried to pull his head down to hurt him in any way I could. I wanted to hold his head against the pavement, push his face into the street. He held my arms and we rolled over, ending with him sitting next to me, my head locked against his side.

"Now say I can't rip your head off."

I couldn't breathe and when I said what I could, he tightened his hold on my neck. It hurt, and it was dark underneath him. I was sweaty. Gasping. The ground was hard and rough, is all I can say.

Then Drew was off me, and when I sat up, Dub held him against the car, his hand on Drew's neck. "It's over," he said. "Now be the fuck out."

I stood up slowly, watching Drew. He looked hurt worse by what Dub had said and done than by anything I did. He had a scrape on the side of his arm and his shirt had stretched out of its shape. He looked around: Jerrod had been his friend first, a guy he met at kung-fu, and he and Dub were close.

"What you looking at?" Dub asked.

"Go on, fuck off," Jerrod yelled, pointing his chin up and at Drew, who didn't say anything. When Drew started away, Jerrod ran up and pushed him from behind, but Drew didn't stop, or turn, or try to fight back.

"I told you I would jump for you," Dub said.

"Yo, you punked that bitch." Jerrod slapped hands with Dub.

Dub punched my shoulder, hard, as I stood up. "That shit was all right." He nodded.

"Fuck was that crazy leg shit?" Jerrod asked me.

I shook my hands and brushed the dirt from my palms. I couldn't really believe the fight had ended. "OK," I said, but it was more like it just came out of my mouth.

They all started walking back toward my house and I followed. They said how they thought it would be worse, that I didn't do so bad, that Drew fought like a pussy.

"It was OK," I said, and Dub clapped his hand around the back of my neck.

"That's right," he said. "Now you in there." He faked like he was going to hit me in the stomach, then laughed when I flinched.

Don Flamenco's finest round

We got inside and went straight to the kitchen. Dub opened the refrigerator door and handed out Cokes. I saw my mom had a wine cooler on the top shelf and reached for it. "Fuck it," I said, twisting the cap.

"Ooh, he big now," Dub said.

"Yo, what's that?" Jerrod asked.

"Wine cooler."

Dub said, "You the man now, I guess."

I took a long drink from the bottle. The liquid was cold and sweet but also sour, like when you leave cider for a long time. But I liked it. I liked drinking in the day like this. I'd had wine coolers before, with Dub when we'd convinced a guy in Harvard Square to buy us a two-liter, and once with my cousin after my bar mitzvah. I'd tasted wine, but this was better. It tasted good, like I had earned it.

Dub held out his hand. I gave him the bottle, and he took a pull. "Nasty," he said. I wiped the top off with my shirt when he handed it back, then drank again. "What was that?" he said.

"What?"

"You see that?" he said to Jerrod.

"That's what I'm talking about," Jerrod said.

"Right."

"See what?" I said.

"That's bullshit."

They went upstairs and I followed. I sat down as they turned on the TV and the Nintendo and Mike Tyson started up. My heart was still racing from everything that had happened, and my left hand was shaking. I felt good though, and it was a hot day, so I took my shirt off to wipe my face. I was sweating pretty hard. I put my shirt down and took a good, long drink from the wine cooler.

"Yo, he fucked your back up," Jerrod said, pointing to my side.

"What?" I said.

"Yo, what is all those marks there?"

I stood up. In the mirror I saw the same gray stretch marks along my left side and up my back that had been there for the past two years, since I grew four inches in sixth grade. "Oh," someone said.

"These are stretch marks." I tried to tell them how the marks just came from all the growing I'd done, and that there wasn't anything I could do about it, that they didn't hurt.

Dub touched my side and said it felt like scales. Then the others wanted to touch it and they did. Jerrod said, "Yo, that's nasty."

I put my shirt back on and sat down behind the others.

On the TV, Dub and Jerrod took turns fighting the first few boxers, Glass Joe and Von Kaiser. Then Dub did his best to fend off Piston Honda, a fighter it'd only taken me a few tries to beat, and in the third round he managed a TKO when Piston Honda was tired. He passed the controller to Jerrod.

"Yo, I'm coming for you, Soda Popinski," Jerrod said, throwing a few jabs.

I drank my wine cooler and sank into a chair in the back of the room, waiting my turn. I could play a lot longer than the others and get all the way to Mike Tyson, but I would use the cheat code now and just go right there.

Don Flamenco's finest round

Jerrod slapped palms with Dub, then snapped his fingers as Don Flamenco was announced on the card.

"You next, pizza man," he said.

The Don Flamenco fight started like it always did: he came out dancing with a rose in his mouth, throwing big punches and looking funny. Then the rose disappeared and he danced in front of Jerrod at the bell. Jerrod pushed buttons, and his boxer, Little Mac, threw a few jabs that the Don blocked. Then he threw a headshot that Don Flamenco dodged. Then the Don threw a jab that caught Little Mac under the chin, sending him flying, and when Jerrod was about to punch, the Don followed it with another jab that connected. Then the outline of the Don's body turned yellow and he started throwing body shots. He hit Jerrod with a right, then a left, both to the ribs, then three successive left jabs connected to Little Mac's face and he dropped his gloves. Don Flamenco went to work on Jerrod's head then, with combinations that kept going until Jerrod was almost out. Don Flamenco followed with two long uppercuts, stretching for the sky, first with his left hand, and then one final blow with the right that dropped Jerrod and Little Mac to the canvas.

Don Flamenco stayed extended, his long, thin right arm held high in the air on his follow-through, his feet barely touching the ground, and his bicep so close to his face that he looked like he was kissing it.

Dub knocked the controller out of Jerrod's hand as the referee started counting. "You got fucked up, kid."

Jerrod tried to hit Dub in the arm at the same time as he picked up the controller.

He started pushing the buttons, trying to get Little Mac off the canvas.

"You best punch those buttons!"

Jerrod tapped the buttons madly, but the referee was already at eight. We could only see the top of Little Mac's head at ten, and then he fell back down. "Knock out! Knock out," the referee said.

Dub laughed. "Yo, you got fucked up!" He pushed Jerrod's head to the side.

I sat up straight, laughing.

"Fucked up," Dub said. "You didn't land a punch." He hit Jerrod on the back.

"I've never seen a beating like that," I said. "You didn't even hit him!" I was laughing hard and easy with Dub at the dismantling. I'd never seen Don Flamenco fight that well. Jerrod even had to smile as the Don started into his dance again with the rose in his mouth, throwing big uppercuts and bringing his arms up so he could kiss his biceps. He danced a few steps to the right, then sidled back the other way.

"Fuck you, Don Flamenco," Jerrod said, holding up his middle finger.

"That's right," I said. "Get mad now."

"Served son."

I held out my hand toward Dub, palm open, and he looked at it. He looked at me and I could tell he was thinking about who I was and what and whether I had any worth in his world. He looked at my hand for just a second, probably, but in that time I imagined a lot of questions I couldn't answer. I watched him.

But then he slapped my palm, just one hit, not too hard, and that was something.

"OK," I said. "OK."

Dub took the controller to start the game up again.

this one thing

"These here are ten, and these are ten and up." My father's new wife Janice—my step-mother—held the two trays of cheap rings over what was left of the salmon and passed the "ten and up" tray to my aunt.

My father dropped his fork.

"These are my newest," Janice said. "I just got them in." She produced a smaller tray of rings, set it down in front of me. "Take a look, Adam," she said. "Maybe there's a girl back at school you're thinking of."

"If I never saw this junk again, I wouldn't mind," my dad said, and laughed. He meant it, I thought, but I couldn't believe he'd said it. My father and Janice had been married since February, when they'd had their "Las Vegas Special", as my mother called it.

"I mean it," he said. "I could do without all of this."

Janice laughed. What else could she do? If it wasn't funny then maybe it wasn't a joke. "How about some rings for you to take back to that girl, Adam?" she said.

"What?" I said. I shook my head. "No."

this one thing

My dad said, "The girls have a thing against jewelry where he goes to college."

"It's not a thing," I said. "It's more an awareness of the roles that women play in our society and how the media controls what we think of their image."

"I like this one," my aunt said. She was pointing to something with a big white face.

Janice said, "That's real enamel, you know."

My father smiled. "Enamel, is it?"

Janice popped the ring out of its holder and presented it. "I can give this to you for wholesale," she said. "Ten dollars. That's a good deal, really. It's more than fair." She put both her hands out on the table. There was a ring on almost every finger.

My mother never wore much jewelry. She lived in Cambridge now, by herself, and always wanted me to come over.

"But choose a few to think about," Janice said. "Here, let me show you more product."

My aunt picked at the tray of rings.

"What do you think of this one?" Janice said. "Wouldn't it look great with that zirconia you're wearing?"

My dad started coughing like he had a fishbone stuck in his throat. "Oh, this," said my aunt, raising her hand to a pendant passed down from my grandmother. "This is diamond."

My father stood and excused himself. "You kids can handle the shopping club without me." My father looked at me and then he nodded at Janice. I started clearing my place.

"Have I showed you the clocks that play sounds from a different national park every hour?" Janice said.

In the kitchen, my father stood bent over with his hands on the sink. "Are you all right?" I asked.

He stood up. The lights were off, but sunlight came in through the windows on the other side of the room. It shone onto the table where we ate our breakfasts, most of the meals that didn't involve company.

"I'm O.K.," he said. "It's just— It's been a long day."

"Did you have enough to eat?" I asked.

"Did I?" he said, putting his hands on his stomach.

For dinner we'd had poached salmon, grilled vegetables on the side. Everyone commented on how good it was, including my father, but it wasn't. It was store-bought. Janice bought food ready-made from a big supermarket out by the highway. Our dinner had come in metal trays that she popped into the oven and then spooned onto platters that had once held my real mother's real cooking.

"I don't know how she does it," my father said. "Your stepmother. All that cooking."

I turned to face the windows. The light on the table was pale, broken into boxes by the window frames. The side of the kitchen where we stood—where the sink faced the stove and the cabinets—held shadows in the afternoon quiet.

"She just had some new flowers put in," my father said. He started toward the door. "When I was outside earlier, I thought I could smell them."

We went outside and he pointed to the three even rows of lilies. "Aren't those nice?"

"They look good," I said. "Who planted them?"

this one thing

"I don't know. She has someone who comes in." My father walked back toward the house and put his foot on the bottom step.

"I took some pretty cool classes this semester," I said.

A soft breeze came through the yard. Our shadows were long, bending up the house toward the windows.

"That must have been nice."

"They were hard."

I wanted to talk to him, tell him things about what I'd learned, ask him things; there was a lot I wondered about, places I wasn't supposed to mention: Atlantic City and Foxwood's, JuJu's and the Alley Cat. My mother had told me these names over the phone but I wanted to hear from my father what he'd been doing. I wanted to know why he married this woman, where he found her.

"What's been going on with you?" I said.

"Larry!" Janice called, from inside. She called his name, and my father started talking about the lilies, but Janice kept yelling, getting closer. He was saying how a man had planted in the garden for a whole morning: how he'd planted the lilies, where he put them, how many rows. We could hear her in the kitchen. I pretended I didn't, that I was listening to my father.

Then, when her face was at the door and she could see us, my father stopped talking. "Where did you go?" Janice said.

"We came outside."

I said, "I thought we could smell the flowers."

"Go back inside, Janice," he said.

Then it was quiet. Janice watched us through the screen, the house dark behind her. Her face looked pale, her head too big for her shoulders, like it was ready to fall off at any moment. She had on dark glasses that made her eyes look deep-set inside their sockets. Her hair shot out at all angles, like a kindergarten drawing of the sun.

My father stood still, looking down at the welcome mat at the bottom of our front stairs.

I counted three breaths as she stood in the doorway. Then she was gone and the door was just dark.

My father put one hand in his pocket and started jangling something. He leaned the other hand on his knee. I could feel him studying my face.

In the garden there were pink lilies and red ones in nice even rows leading up toward the house. Over by the fence, my father had put in one of those wooden ducks on a pole, the kind with wings that spin in the wind.

"So tell me about your first year of college," he said.

"It was good," I said. I wanted to tell him everything I'd learned in Professor Thompson's class on 20th Century thought, how everything had seemed so clear-cut the way he explained what was wrong with our country, how it was all due to the hegemonic powers of the media.

"Did you learn anything?" he said.

"I had a great class where we learned about society, and about how the media manipulates us."

"Did Janice tell you about her winning streak in Las Vegas?" My father asked. "Or our trip to Alaska?"

"No," I said. I shook my head and he started talking to me about their flight to Vancouver and their cruise up the Pacific Corridor to the Glacier National Land Trust. He said they'd seen ice floes hanging huge as buildings and frozen turquoise ponds. As he started in about Fairbanks, I heard Janice clomping through the kitchen. She came out onto the porch with her hands raised.

"Larry, she's buying the rings in there," she said. "She really likes them!" Her mouth opened wide when she talked and I could see she was excited. She pointed to the rings on her fingers. "I gave her one like this for ten but the one like this I had to ask fifteen for."

My father shook his head. "You don't charge my sister, Janice. Those should be gifts," he said. "Our gifts to her, Janice."

"But Larry," she said. "It's like I'm not even charging her."

My father shook his head. "No, Janice."

"But those are good deals," she said. "The same prices I paid."

My father brought his hand up and pointed back to the house. "You go back in there—" He started to say something else, but then Janice tilted her head, just slightly, looking at him. She looked at him, and then she looked at his hand, the outstretched finger. I heard a car drive by. My father lowered his arm, put his hand in his pocket.

I turned away from the house and walked onto the lawn, toward the garage. The grass was still wet from my father running the sprinkler and I could see the water making dark spots on my sneakers. I put my hands on the back of a folding chair. The backside of the garage was a blank slate of concrete now. All through high school, the garage had been one big cube of green leaves—this side a wall of concrete covered with ivy—but then last summer my father had had it stripped clean. He said the vines were tearing apart the garage.

"Are you going to pay me for those rings?" Janice said, behind me. "Or are you going to say you will now but then try to start a whole other argument about it later?"

Around the base of the garage the gardener's ivy-killer had burned away the grass, and it had not grown back: a yellow strip stretched onto the lawn for maybe a foot of ruined, destroyed grass. Perhaps nothing would ever grow back there.

"Janice," my father said. I turned around in time to see him close his eyes and pass his hand over his face. "For me," he said, "Right now. Can you just do this one thing?"

Then Janice was quiet and I heard the wind blow through the backyard and the wings on my father's wooden duck start to spinning. They sounded like a kid's bike with cards in the spokes of the tires.

It seemed as if something sorry passed between them, and then Janice nodded and started up the stairs again, her shoes striking the hollow wood as she went.

My father produced a pack of cigarettes and started slapping it against his palm. He came onto the lawn to stand next to me.

"So tell me more about school," he said, taking out a cigarette.

I turned to look at him. It had been a long time since I'd seen my father smoking. I couldn't remember the last time. With the cigarette in his mouth, my father looked like someone I didn't know. In the way he was dressed he resembled my father, he stood the same way: hands on his waist and pants pulled up over his hips. But this was somebody different, someone who haggled over prices with this woman, Janice, someone who had shown up in a house where my father had once lived.

"I thought I learned a lot this year in my classes," I said. "Toward the end I thought I had it all figured out."

He nodded, took another drag.

"I got good grades."

My father's eyes were dull, with something going on behind them that didn't involve me, this lawn, or our garden.

I turned back to the garage, trying to remember anything from Professor Thompson's lectures to tell my father: how the media was ruining our lives, or who wrote our book about the destructive nature of television, but I couldn't think. The garage wall had marks on it, like tan-lines, left behind from where the ivy had attached itself. They angled across the wall in odd patterns, making jagged lines without any order.

"I have to go inside," I said. "I think there's something I need to go look at."

My father nodded. He took the cigarette out of his mouth and waved toward the house. "I'll just stay out here for a few minutes," he said.

I went inside and up the back stairs to my room, and closed the door. Janice was still talking in the dining room, but with the door closed I couldn't hear her words, just sounds. I could see my father through the window, still standing on the lawn, smoking his cigarette. He looked up at our house, but I don't think he could see in.

On my desk, the textbooks I'd brought back from college

stood in a stack. I sat down in front of them, read the titles along the spines. They seemed like things from a foreign place now, a place where there'd never been a time when I rode on my father's shoulders, or we did abdominal exercises together in the hall. But here they were in my old room, on a desk next to my old life-sized poster of Kevin McHale. He stood with a stupid grin, holding a little, lunch-room-sized carton of milk, looking like an idiot, framed by my old NFL wallpaper. I could smell my father's cigarette smoke coming in through the window.

I closed the blinds.

responsibility

Adam noticed Vaughn sitting on his mother's front steps when he turned into her driveway. Vaughn sat smoking, and didn't move as Adam parked. Vaughn was his mother's boyfriend now, and lived with her, but Adam had only met him twice: once over Christmas, and once when he first got home for the summer, about three weeks before.

"It's good to see you," Vaughn said, holding out a pack of Camels when Adam got out. Adam had reached the point where cigarettes didn't nauseate him anymore. He'd started to like them even: they were good for time management on the long nights at his summer job with Emerson Electric and the long days without Sarah. He took one and closed the door of his father's car.

"Your mother will be excited you're here," Vaughn said.

Adam thought he could smell the booze on Vaughn's breath, but he knew his mother and Vaughn weren't drinking, that Vaughn was supposed to have quit.

"Well?" Vaughn said, his eyes bright behind his thin glasses and his mouth open wide enough for Adam to see his molars. Vaughn looked directly at him, like he was trying to meld their souls.

"Thanks?"

"OK," Vaughn said. Adam turned away from him, avoiding the gaze he couldn't return. Across the street was a house with a yard he'd once played in. He remembered the upstairs family's son, a boy named Phil. Most recently, Adam heard Phil was off doing something other than college, something that involved a garage. Now in the yard the hoop was bent like someone had been hanging on it, and the net was missing, too. No one had played there in some time.

Vaughn stood up and patted Adam's shoulder. He tilted his head. "I like you, Adam," he said. "I think we can be buddies, me and you." He let his jaw drop after each word, his mouth wide open. "How would you feel about that?"

There was an enthusiasm in Vaughn's eyes that Adam couldn't match—they sparkled, as if he thought they could really be pals. "That sounds all right?"

Vaughn inhaled, watching through thin eyes, and then turned away to blow out smoke. "Good," he said. He brought the cigarette below his knee and rubbed it between his thumb and finger until the lit cherry fell onto the stoop. After rubbing out the rest of the tobacco, he dropped the filter into his shirt pocket.

"You want to see a trick?" Vaughn said. He dug his hand into the pocket of his shorts and brought it out with a rubber thumb. Adam could tell it was supposed to look like skin, but it was too light—it looked like it was made out of canvas.

responsibility

"Do you like magic?" Vaughn said.

Adam looked away from the thumb, at his mother's Corolla parked in front of the house: Vaughn's Taurus was just behind it.

"Can I have your cigarette," Vaughn said. "You're done with that, aren't you?"

Adam took a last drag and passed the cigarette to Vaughn.

"Nothing in my hands, right?" Vaughn showed his palms and turned his hands over, holding the cigarette between his fingers. The thumb was even more evident now. "And now," Vaughn said. He made a fist with his other hand and stuck the rubber thumb in. The real thumb came out uncovered, then Vaughn took a quick drag of Adam's cigarette, and pushed it into his fist. "Always have to be careful here," he said, wincing. He pushed his real thumb in behind the cigarette and opened his hands wide.

"Gone!" Vaughn held his palms up, then clapped once. They were empty, the rubber thumb back where it had begun and the cigarette inside it.

Adam tried to look like he was surprised and enjoying himself, as if he was young enough to appreciate this.

"And now where do you think that cigarette is?" Vaughn said.

Adam checked behind his ears. "It's not behind my ears."

"What?"

"It's not behind my ears," Adam said, and Vaughn stopped smiling. "I don't have it," Adam said. He showed his empty palms to Vaughn.

"You saw the thumb, didn't you?"

"What thumb?"

"You saw it," Vaughn said. He wrung his hands together and the cigarette was in his palm, snubbed out and bent into a Z. He dropped it and clapped the ashes off his hands, stuck the rubber thumb back into his pocket. "You saw the thumb and you didn't say anything," he said. "You let me go on with that trick like an asshole."

"What thumb?"

Vaughn stood and brushed off his shorts. "Forget it!" he said. "Just forget it!" He went inside then, up the stairs onto the porch and through the screen door. Adam watched him disappear into the house, then got up and followed him. Vaughn was already up the stairs to Adam's mother's half of the house—the second and third floors. He started as soon as he got to the landing. "Your son doesn't like magic!" he said.

Adam noticed a new picture on the wall. In it, his mother and Vaughn were smiling, pulling for control of a long-handled metal spatula, the kind you would use with an outdoor grill. Vaughn had his hands on the handle, but Adam's mother had both hers on his wrists. Her face was tan and happy, her short hair being blown by some vacation breeze.

"What are you talking about?" Adam's mother said. She came out of the living room wearing a shirt that Adam had given her for her birthday when he was fourteen. She smiled but tried to hide it by keeping her mouth closed, but her happiness spread up into her face, making her eyes beam and glisten.

"Adder," she said. "Do you see what shirt I'm wearing?"

Her face was young; there was something about her eyes that men always noticed. Guys had been telling Adam that his mother had great eyes since she left his father ten years before.

responsibility

At first they were good guys, money-earners with careers, but as time went on their résumés weakened. Vaughn seemed an improvement over the last couple of losers, however, simply by the fact that he was Adam's mother's own age.

But Adam knew his mother liked Vaughn: the night after they first met, his mother had called to ask what Adam thought, and he told her he liked him, that Vaughn had seemed all right. "I'm so glad you said that," she'd said. "You know, it's been a while since I've felt this good about anybody. And Vaughn really likes me. He tells me." She was almost giddy. "It's so cool."

She said this and Adam had listened. He listened to her explain how Vaughn made her feel especially wanted, a feeling she had never really had, she said, not even with his father, and when she finished he told her he thought that was great. He said it was good to see her happy, that that was his only concern.

And now she stood in front of him smiling, asking him who'd given her the shirt they both knew he had, standing next to a picture of herself and Vaughn.

"I gave you that shirt when I was in the eighth grade, Mom," Adam said.

"Right. That's why I love it." She smiled. "Because my son gave it to me." She waved her arms toward her. "Come up. Come up," she said. "We're finished with dinner, but we're just going to have ice cream. Can you stay for a little while?"

When Adam reached the top of the stairs, she reached out and touched his wrist, making a circle around it with her first finger and her thumb.

Adam pulled away. He looked at his mother and then at Vaughn, the two of their faces quiet, standing next to the picture of them laughing. "I could stay for some ice cream," he said.

She padded into the kitchen in her slippers. "You two are going to get the best sundaes you've ever had," she said. "My two handsome men."

Adam went into the living room and sat on the couch; Vaughn came in and sat across from him, on his mother's favorite chair. "How's the nightshift going?" Vaughn asked.

"Fine."

"Just fine? Things have been big business down at the lot," Vaughn said. He smiled and waved his hands in front of his face, then started in about his sales commissions and how, just that afternoon, he had all but "sealed the deal" on a new Explorer with a guy he had known from his old days.

"He's always owed me since I introduced him to his wife," Vaughn said. He crossed his legs and leaned back—his shorts fell back to show Adam the pale, hairy undersides of his thighs.

"She was my girlfriend first, you understand," Vaughn was saying. "Used to follow me around when I was in the band." He uncrossed his legs and then re-crossed them on the other side. Adam looked away. "I got to know her pretty good at first, before we were dating, but then when we started going together we found out it wouldn't work."

Vaughn leaned forward, put his hands on the coffee table. "She couldn't handle me," he said, shaking his head. He leaned back, gesturing toward his lap. "I'm a big man," he said. Adam cuffed the back of his neck and looked up at the ceiling. He massaged the two rods below his skull. "It's different with your mother though, she—"

"Enough," Adam said, closing his eyes. "Jesus Christ it's enough, Vaughn. Let's just not talk anymore."

When Adam opened his eyes, Vaughn was looking at him with his head tilted expectantly. "Adam? I'm really sorry, pal. I totally apologize for what I said. Sorry." He held up his empty palms as if the hidden cigarette might still be an issue.

"I'm sorry," he said.

Adam pointed toward the kitchen with his chin. "That's my mother," he said. She came in, carrying bowls of ice cream, as Vaughn raised his shoulders. His face was plain, empty.

Adam's mother sat next to him on the couch. "It's good to see you," she said. She handed Adam a heaping bowl of ice cream, topped with hot fudge, and reached her arm around his shoulders. "Remember when you used to eat whipped cream right out of the can?" she asked.

"I still do."

She laughed, and Adam ate his ice cream. He managed a smile. "I'm taking this great class on grooming Bonsai trees," she said. "I'll finally start my Japanese garden!"

"That's great, Mom."

Vaughn asked who she was taking the class with, and Adam's mother said his cousin, Deb. She started talking about how Deb had moved back up to Boston after art school and was living with a guy she'd been dating.

Vaughn was shoveling big spoons of hot fudge and ice cream into his mouth. "You should go see her," Adam's mother said. She wiped hot fudge from the side of his bowl with her finger, then licked it off.

"I thought she broke up with that guy," Adam said.

His mother nodded. "They're back together now. Call her. She'd love to hear from you." She went in the other room and brought back his cousin's number.

"Call her," she said.

Adam spooned up the last he could eat of his ice cream and set the bowl on the table. He stood. "I should go."

"It was good to see you," Adam's mother said. "Let me give you a hug." Vaughn was still eating. "That's good," she said. "My Adder."

Vaughn placed his bowl on the coffee table and stood up.

"Call me this week," Adam's mother said.

Vaughn offered his hand and Adam took it. "My two handsome men," his mother said again.

Adam went downstairs and let himself out. He bought a pack of Parliaments and smoked two on the drive home. After a third in his room, he called Deb. "Hold on?" she said. Her hand muffled the phone. When she came back on, there was less noise in the background. "Can I talk to you about something?" she said.

Adam heard a door close on her end. "Vaughn?" he asked.

"Vaughn," she said. He closed his eyes and waited to hear what came next. "I went to your mom's last week and he told me that I've gained too much weight," she said.

Adam tapped another cigarette out of the box.

"Too much for who?"

responsibility

"So I told him he was an asshole," she said. "I couldn't believe he would talk to me like that and I told my mother and she said it isn't fair for some idiot to keep me from seeing my own aunt, but now I don't like to go over there because he's an ass."

Adam knocked the filter end of a cigarette against his desk.

"What did my mom say?"

"What can she do? My mom talked to her. She said she'd talk to him. Maybe she talked to him. Maybe he's too much of an idiot to hear anything she says." Deb grunted, getting ready to say something. "It's embarrassing," she said, finally. "Don't you think he's embarrassing your mom?"

Adam switched the phone to his other ear. "It's bad," he said. "I know." He tasted the cigarette and got ready to light it. He wanted to like Vaughn; he wanted Vaughn to be a good guy and for everything to be great for his mom. He did want these things. Adam saw his mother and Vaughn in the photo they had on the wall, the one where they were laughing.

"I should go," Deb said. "Josh and I are in the middle of a movie."

"Okay."

"Call me again and we'll hang out!"

"Okay," he said. He hung up the phone.

His mother had gone from one boyfriend to another after the divorce, lowering her standards by degrees with each one. She reacted as if every failure were her fault—as if her mistakes came in trying to be with men who were better than she. In a short amount of time she'd come to this.

On the wall at his desk were Adam's old pictures. He looked at the picture of Sarah. In the picture, she wears a black tank-top and leans forward, holding the shirt up to her chest so that only a thin line of cleavage shows. She has dark lipstick on and her long, curly black hair falls all around her face. Her smile looks genuinely happy. If they were still together, Adam thought, he'd have more to do than go to work and visit his mother. The whole summer would've been completely different. He'd have been happy.

The other picture on Adam's wall was of his mother and father when he was little, when they were still together. They stand next to their old car in somebody's driveway in the picture, Adam's mother holding him, his head in the crook of her arm. She leans toward his father, wearing a denim summer dress with a paisley patch over her chest. Her hair is shorter and her face younger, and she looks a little confused, as if she isn't sure where she is, but she looks good, healthy. His dad has on a denim blazer with patches at the elbows and a wide brown tie. His has long hair and grins.

Those were different times, Adam knew, and his mother had come through a lot. She was on her own now and there was something she needed from Vaughn, but before she met him she had been all right. She had taken Adam to a nursery in Concord the previous summer, and seemed happy in her independence.

The weather had been nice that day, not too hot, though it was summer. She drove them out to the country and took Adam to the back of the nursery, where a long table of Bonsai trees stood behind all the other plants. Each of the Bonsai was potted in a shiny porcelain pot with a Japanese character painted on its side. His mother had chosen one in a purple base. The tree looked delicate: its trunk curved to one side with a small wooden splint supporting it.

responsibility

"Isn't it beautiful?"

"I guess so," he said, but she was right: there was something unique and tragic about the tree. She picked up its purple pot and looked at the bottom, judging the size. Adam touched it, felt the raise where the letter was printed. He fingered the strange shapes.

"Do you think I could take care of this?" she asked.

He nodded. "Sure, you could, Mom."

She put the tree down and stood back to look at it. "I could," she said.

She bought her first Bonsai that afternoon after talking to the man who worked there about how she could transfer it into her backyard in the summer and how much light to give it in the winter. He told her to buy special shears to keep it the right shape and size and she asked Adam about them—if she should buy the ones with the blue handles or the red—and he told her the red, which were the ones that she chose.

Adam shut off the light and sat at his desk in the dark, watching the headlights of passing cars illuminate the walls around him in rectangular ghosts. When he was ready, he went outside and sat behind the wheel of his father's car, holding the keys. He put a cigarette in his mouth, lit it, and turned the ignition.

The drive from Newton to Cambridge was familiar terrain for Adam; he'd done it enough times that he could make it now without thinking, almost without paying any attention to the road. He drove mindlessly until he came to to his mother's turn, but then he kept going. He passed the old hospital, and the new one, and the turn he had taken all through high school to get to where Sarah lived. He drove down her street and looked to see if the light was on in her bedroom. Last he'd heard, she was going to B.U. and living with her parents, but that could have changed. Her room was dark.

He came to a turn that led back toward his mother's and took it. These were the old streets he'd learned to drive on, with his mother beside him and Sarah in the back seat. Just once he had looked back at her—a quick smile to tell Sarah he was doing it—and his mother had had to grab the wheel. She surprised him, but he turned back in time to see the car come within a foot of hitting the phone pole.

After a little while, he came to his mother's street and parked in front of her house, behind Vaughn's car. A light was on in the top floor window—the room that used to be Adam's —and another was on in the kitchen.

He didn't have a key anymore, so he rang the bell then waited while his mother came down the stairs, her heaviness creaking the wood at each step. She wore her nightgown. "Adam," she said. "Is everything all right?"

Adam shook his head, moving past her. "This is because I love you, Mom," he said and headed upstairs.

"What? What is because you love me?" she said, behind him. "What are you talking about, Adam?"

"Wait here."

He went upstairs past the living room where her book lay open on the couch and kept going, to the third floor, where he knew Vaughn would be. He could hear noises coming from the TV, like some inhuman yelling.

In what used to be his bedroom, Vaughn was asleep on the

futon, the remote control balanced on his leg. On TV, a creature with a hairy face, covered with dirt, bared its teeth and then made a sound like an animal screaming. Adam shut it off.

"Adam," Vaughn said, opening his eyes. He rubbed his hands over his eyelids and sat up, scratching the back of his head.

"Stand up," Adam said.

Vaughn patted his thighs and put the remote control down next to him. "What's wrong?" he asked. "What's going on?"

"Stand up."

Vaughn put his hands on his knees and stood. He offered Adam his hand and smiled. "It's good to see you," he said. "There's a good movie—"

"Take off your glasses."

"What?"

"Take them off." Adam felt like he wouldn't be able to say anything else, that he needed a cigarette. He closed his eyes and opened them, still standing where he was.

"What's the problem?"

Adam swallowed. "Please take off your glasses, Vaughn."

He heard his mother coming up the stairs, her steps heavy and slow. "What's going on up here?" she said.

Vaughn took off his glasses. His face had never seemed so big; Adam could see every wrinkle around Vaughn's eyes, every white hair along the sides of his head, behind his temples. His mouth was open; Adam could see his fillings.

Adam's mother was behind them, breathing hard. "Stay downstairs, Mom? Please?" Adam hadn't wanted her to come up, had forgotten about Vaughn's glasses and now just wanted to get the whole thing over with. It wasn't supposed to be this way. His arms felt heavy, like they were thin ropes suspending rocks from his shoulders.

"I just need to talk to Vaughn for a few minutes." Adam put his hands on his hips, which felt like an exercise he could barely finish.

"But—"

"It's all right," Vaughn said. "We'll be down soon."

She nodded and started toward the stairs.

Adam turned back to Vaughn. He seemed much thinner and shorter than Adam had expected. His face was a few inches lower, but just in front of Adam's. "Take off your glasses."

"I did," Vaughn said. He had his glasses in his hand.

Adam heard the door to the downstairs bathroom close. He opened his hands and clenched them into fists that felt like doorknobs.

"I don't hit people," Adam said. "But I'm supposed to, aren't I?"

Vaughn shook his head, and Adam's arms felt heavy, like he wanted to rest them by putting his hands in his pockets, but he knew that was not something he could do.

"For what you've done."

Vaughn nodded. "Yes," he said. "I understand, but no." He shook his head. "What're you talking about?"

"What you're doing here."

"Adam," Vaughn said, shaking his head. "Let me ask you, do you know how much I love your mother?"

Adam felt something slipping away from him, like his

chance at a significant decision had passed. He was beyond what he understood and this was not at all what he wanted. He opened his eyes and closed them, trying to see what he was supposed to do.

"Adder?" Vaughn said, putting his hand on Adam's shoulder.

And that was when Adam hit him.

It wasn't the good kind of punch that'd knock someone out in a bar—this all happened like something that Adam was only watching, like on television—but his fist caught Vaughn on the chest, below his neck, and knocked him back. Vaughn's body doubled and he dropped on the floor with some noise, landing against a chair. His hands were down by his sides and his glasses slid under the bed. His eyes opened and shut like he wasn't sure what he was seeing.

"You don't do these things," Adam said. He tried to point at Vaughn but could see it looked stupid, like something from a bad movie. "These kind of things are not what people say here, not what they do," he said.

Vaughn shook his head.

Adam's mother called from downstairs, "What was that noise?"

"If you have respect," Adam said. He pressed the palm of his hand against his eye, letting himself see the dark stars for a moment.

"You should respect her," he tried, and Vaughn was starting to get himself together. He looked up at Adam and his eyes were empty, as if he was unsure of what to do.

Adam turned and walked back to the top of the stairs. He could see his mother at the bottom, just starting up. "What was that noise?" she said. "Adam, what did you do?"

Adam started down the stairs. When he came to his mother, he tried to move past her to get down the stairs to the front door where he could have a cigarette and get away from all this, but she was blocking the way. She put her arms around him from the side and held him.

"What did you do, Adam? What's wrong?"

"You're better than this, mom." Adam lifted his arms as high as she'd let them, and held his mother around the waist. "You're better than this because I love you."

"Adder?" she said. "What happened?"

He pulled her to him and held on.

"Vaughn?" she said, calling up the stairs. "What was that noise, Adam?" she asked. She let go of him and started up the stairs, looking for Vaughn.

Nilsa

Believe that the world is governed by an elaborate system of checks and measures, that life is meted out in a zero-sum game —every pleasure balanced by an equal and opposite pain, everything earned. This is what I used to feel when I was living scared in The City, when drum and bass was becoming a religion and I was taking what I could from every moment, more than I ever deserved, digging my own hole.

We started at Thomas', snorting a white powder we poured out of capsules and mashed smooth with a flashlight. He said it was something he'd been passed as e, but we knew it wasn't. Crank is what it probably was. We sucked it into our noses through a rolled dollar bill off a newspaper. And when I went outside I realized that the city had become as dark and as quiet as a diving bell.

A cab ride that took us through the streets underwater— just the tops of the light posts sticking into the air, their dim glow seeping down into our mire—and then we arrived at Twilo and made our way through the line. I saw her inside, in the wide-open first area, with the dance room on our left and the hall to everything else straight ahead of us, kids filing in all around us, screaming with their clothes who they wanted people to think they really were. Her friend talked to Thomas. She surprised me because she looked back, as if it was all right that I stared. Most times they never looked back, acted like I did something to them and walked in the other direction, but not her. She smiled.

Thomas slipped a white pill in my hand; he said, "This e comes on slow. Let me know when you're rolling and we'll take the a."

Looking at her, I took it, trying to decide what she was or who she thought I was, until she said, "Hi."

"Hi."

Her red lips spread wide, showing white teeth and a tiny gap in the middle. Her mouth might have been just like any other, but her smile was different, like then and there she knew how everything would happen between us and she didn't hold it against me, not for a second, not for the world.

I told her my name and she said, "I'm Nilsa," and she was still smiling, or maybe she was smiling again, but probably she never had stopped.

"What are you taking?" I said.

She brought her eyelids down and then up again, showed me her green eyes, and said, "Nothing." She was clean and I was where I was—there was nothing I could do about it then.

All around us kids rode their highs, wearing baggy pants and tight tank tops. The music was bright basslines I couldn't get my head around—looping beats pulling me in. Like she was touching a tender sunburn, Nilsa cupped her breast and laughed. She said, "I got this pierced today. It feels funny."

Nilsa

Disco balls blazed patterns on the walls all around us and snapshots of colors exploded on the back of my eyelids in the minutes that elapsed while I blinked.

"Do you want to see it?" she said.

I nodded, moving into her eyes, feeling myself swimming in their green.

She held her shirt down from the neck and showed me there, in the middle of Twilo, surrounded by the streams of others: her nipple, as brown and red as any other, erect with a curve of metal running through it to end in two silver balls. My face and glimpses of my future shimmered back in its small round circles; there were canyons reflected on that metal, divine heights and visions of red rivers. I tried to crawl back into her eyes when this was gone, but now I was on the outside with her, the two of us together, more comfortable than I could ever ask you to believe.

Thomas appeared, and I asked him, "Did you see that?"

"You're rolling," he said.

My hands had started moving with the bassline and I brought one up to show him. Steam seeped slowly from the walls around us, and lights in the dance room flashed across drag queens on stilts.

"She's Nilsa," I said.

"Cool." Thomas passed me the acid and held it still in my palm as if to pull out all my apprehensions with his breathing, and he did. Or something had. At that moment, I wanted everything; I let go of believing in any future and hoped for divinity in what was around me, praying that everything I'd come to would change, that I'd be released forever from the system of measures and balances that I'd come to believe in; that I'd be saved.

I ate the tab, tasting the bitter, as Nilsa held my hand. I told her how I was a students in the Art Students' League, and that I wanted to make beauty; she led me back into her eyes like it was my return to the womb.

And then later, with the a coming on strongest, Nilsa pressed a bottle of water in my hand and asked me how did I feel? Her eyes beamed green, like I already told you; she smiled brighter than anyone I have ever met, like I told you as well; she did these things, and I told her, "I feel fine."

We wound up on a couch in the dance room. "Do you know what I studied in high school?" she asked.

I closed my eyes and saw melting checkerboards dripping into canyons of brilliant waterfalls following rainbows in front of my face.

"Massage," said Nilsa. "I studied massage."

She went to work on my back then, doing things I felt in seven different languages of feeling, things I knew even then would corrupt how I'd react to everything that ever existed after—in life. "Stop," I begged. I turned around and put my lips against hers, kissed her, whispering, "It can't be this good."

She touched my eyelids with her fingertips and turned me around, kissing my neck and rubbing my back again, stretching the colors out of my muscles and away from my spine. I felt the strong in her hands and the story they were telling me: how she came to NYU from a small town in Japan called Toyohashi, about a three-hour drive south of Tokyo, and how her father

Nilsa

was from Brazil—a man who'd come to work for Mazda and met her mother, gave her a daughter and left her alone to teach Nilsa Japanese and some English, a little Portuguese in case she ever caught up with her old man.

Believe me when I tell you, I knew all of this from her hands.

• • •

We were dancing when the DJ stopped. People cheered and we left into the cold gray sun. Everyone looked pale in the light, like just-born marsupials that hadn't grown fur. Thomas handed me my sunglasses: colored yellow lenses that transformed the world. Electric sidewalks gleamed in the sunlight, grains of glass in the concrete sparkling in the sun as if—tourists from Twilo —we had arrived and found the streets of New York paved with gold.

Thomas and the others filed into cabs, headed for more of his white capsules as Nilsa and I started walking, unsure where we were headed, but going downtown. On Seventh Avenue we stopped at a Rite Aid and she led me inside onto the soft blue carpet. A miracle of sensations greeted us under the brilliance of those fluorescent lightbulbs as we walked the beautiful aisles searching for sweets. The sad-faced cashier knew our names and our predicament; he winked his assurance of my visions. Everywhere around me were small packages with pictures; letters and products radiated from the shelves. The laundry detergents drew me into the red in a bottle of Tide, and I wasn't powerless, but I was held there. I knew then if I saw that much for the rest of my life I'd be crazy, but it'd be in every way worth it. The reds in that Tide were redder than the brightest tomatoes, Clorox blues glistened under those lights not brighter, but more than anything I have ever known; there was more in those colors than I've ever been aware of.

"Can we go?" Nilsa asked.

"It's just that I never stop to enjoy any of the colors like this," I said. "Like they're all right here right now, and so vibrant. That's the perfect word to use for it," I told her. "Vibrant."

"Do you see all this?" I asked her.

She pulled my hand and put her lips up to my cheek. "Is it beautiful?" she asked.

• • •

How Nilsa led me home, I'll never understand, but it was when we were standing in my bedroom naked, but not touching, that I heard it start to rain. I knew then that the rain would last through the weekend, and I understood that the world would take back what I'd stolen with drugs in the night.

For hours afterwards, my mind was a knocked-down power line, flailing and churning out the remnants of break beats and rhythms, thinking in different directions, spouting out currents of thought.

Nilsa's body was hairless and small and gray, still cold from the walk and salt-lined from sweating, with ribs I could pinch between my fingers and a flat stomach that sloped to a small patch of hair. The silver hoop hung from her swollen red nipple.

Outside the rain fell louder and the sound of wet tires slashed clear from the street. My upstairs neighbor rose from his bed and walked to his bathroom above our heads. When he flushed, the water blasted through pipes in my walls. I touched Nilsa's shoulder and felt my fingers on her rubbery skin. Together we crawled into my bed, burrowing under the covers and moving against each other for warmth. As scientists run gentle fingers over specimens, we touched each other silently, browsing in solitude. I ran my fingers up her stomach and traced the curve of her breast, felt the tender pucker of her nipple and the place where the hoop ended in balls. Carefully, my fingertip just fit in between.

She rolled over, sliding her back against my chest and I wrapped my arms around her. With my eyes closed I could still see the checkerboards, but now melted further, their colors faded to darker than before.

I asked her would she let me draw the world on her back then, and though the rain persisted, as if to remind me that this all would end so soon, so suddenly, I pushed on, hoping. I pressed my lips against her shoulder, felt the soft of her skin— smooth like its purpose was to glide against mine, as if there should never be friction between us—and I believed I could give her something there that would help us from then on and forever, that she could be the one I would save.

I collected a few pens from what I could reach on the windowsill—two blues and a black—and I started slow, letting the little metal rollers find their way along her pores. The ink reached out like tiny blue hands, spreading into her skin's valleys as I held the tip to her, and then, starting around her spine, I drew what I could of the visions, just a few boxes, but her contours transformed my lines into curves that became blades of grass spreading out toward her sides, not boxes or checkerboards, but organic fluid shapes. As if I were watching the pen lead my hand, I saw her skin become a blue-lined garden of liquid flowers. Blue daffodils blossomed on her back and down along her hips; her entire spine was a vine of plants and flowers created by God. Everything He created spread out toward her sides. What I beheld was amazing, more beauty than I could ever hope to imagine.

I lay looking at a single flower close to her elbow, its petals opened wide as if it were next to the sun, and I drew one there on her bone, as if this could be all that we needed: a sun.

"We're OK now," I said.

"It's still raining."

Nilsa was shivering and I cupped my hand over her stomach, feeling her breathing take my arm in and out. After a time, the long breaths began, and I asked her if she was asleep. She moved her head just a little and I knew she was crying, that she had wanted me to save her as much as I had wanted to be saved.

"I'm here," I said. It was all I could do for either of us.

• • •

Some few days later, high on ketamine with the sky broken open above us, we sat in Washington Square Park watching the world tear itself to pieces, and she pulled her sleeve down to reveal a fresh-scabbed tattoo on her shoulder. It looked like sperm swimming end to end, touching together to make a letter from four little ribbons. This, in black ink on her shoulder, in the exact place I'd kissed her that first night, our beautiful morning. But the ink wasn't mine, and this was something I'd never have done.

"What is this," I said, running my finger over the scabs.

She said, "It's everything. It's us. It's you."

Nilsa

"It's you?" I asked her. Her skin felt cold and my mind was blurry from the drugs. When she stayed quiet, I asked, "Is it made of sperm?"

She nodded. "It's made of dreams," she said. "Wishes of what we can have."

"Who put this on you?" I said.

She looked up as if to witness the world, and I can believe she was watching angels dance love songs among the clouds, or she could have been watching nothing, the wind.

Across the park a man sat on the benches, disheveled and alone. He looked at the ground like he'd lost something, but he didn't move. Like he knew it could never be found, I saw him reach into his pockets and fish around, then blow his nose into an empty hand.

And when Nilsa touched my fingers I knew that what I'd had of her was gone, that, even if it had all been real in the beginning, it was far from true then. My fingers traced the lines that formed her little tattoo: four black sperm, one little letter. Even bumped on ketamine I couldn't believe what I saw.

She said my name then, and I thought of that first morning, how beautifully pure we had seemed, and I didn't cry, though I wish I could have. I didn't even cry for the world. I knew everything that was wrong with us, the list that stretched for miles up above me and into the heavens; I knew that I'd be out of her life before the scabs of her tattoo even healed. She wasn't going to save me and I couldn't save her; the two of us together couldn't even save that one morning.

But.

But still: if I told you I wouldn't do it all over, or that I never go back to Twilo or spend mornings in Washington Square Park just looking for her, you'd be wrong to believe me.

one of her good nights

At night, Elizabeth Richard would often hold her husband's hand when he was eating and sometimes she would even feed him with the spoon, but there were occasions, she called these his good nights, when he was able to manage on his own. She could tell by the shaky way Tom passed his hand over the top of his head, straightening what little was left of his thin brown hair, that this would not be one of those.

Regis was hounding another contestant into second guessing himself on TV, while Tom arched the spoon up and placed it into his mouth, took it out, and carefully moved his jaw. It was only soup, what his doctors advised to keep his mouth-work minimal. Soup, what he had eaten little other than since his Parkinson's reached this stage of advancement. But soup was still a challenge, enough to keep them both busy.

There had been a time when they sat in the dining room and ate steak for dinner, talking, when she and Tom would never have watched a program like Who Wants to Be a Millionaire, but now there was a real need for voices in their small house, and they'd become less choosy. Especially at night, when the house was quietest, they treated the TV as if it were a long-lost friend, sitting rapt in front of it, letting it make their conversation.

When the doorbell rang, the next potential millionaire was consulting with his brother in Illinois over which US state had the most water area in lakes. Elizabeth looked at Tom, who peered up at her through his spiky eyebrows. He rattled his spoon against the side of his bowl as the doorbell rang again.

She slid her feet into her slippers, and as they sat and listened for it to come once more, the brother in Illinois told his ideas about Minnesota versus, possibly, Maine. When the doorbell rang for a third time, she said, "I'll just get it and find out then."

She got up and, smoothing out her shorts and checking the pins in her hair, crossed in front of the couch, out of the living room, and passed through the front hall to the door. Through the spy hole she could see Adam, their paperboy, standing on the porch. He was facing away from her, with his shoulders hunched, but she could recognize his mackinaw and hat as the garments she had seen hanging out of the car that came down their street early in the morning. She was usually awake to hear the approaching sound of the papers slapping onto porches, and, by the time he was to their house, she was often looking down into the street from Tom's study to see the familiar arm protrude from the window and fling its delivery.

She opened the door and he turned around, as if startled. He dropped his hands behind his back and made an odd face, as if he'd just swallowed something whole. Then he coughed and the smoke came out of his mouth. "Sorry," he said, stooping to brush out his cigarette against their steps. "I didn't realize you were home."

Elizabeth watched him stand up to his full height before she addressed him. "This must be about your Christmas bonus, is that right?"

Adam took his hat off and held it in both hands in front of his chest. "Yes, it is, ma'am."

Always the same thing around this time of year. Very much more of the same. "Well come inside," she said. "Come in and sit while I write you out a check."

He took off his coat and hung it on the rack inside the door, then bent down and unlaced his boots. She noticed it when he looked at her legs once, then twice, while he was crouched down on the floor. This did not bother her: it actually had the opposite effect, made her feel better, a little, as if the work she did on the stairclimber hadn't all gone for nothing.

She even found herself humming slightly as she led Adam into the living room and introduced him to her husband. She saw how Tom did his best to look up at the boy and offered his feeble hand. Adam took the hand as if afraid he might break it and called Tom, "Mr. Richard."

Still facing his tray, Tom looked up at Adam through his eyebrows. He said, "How are you?"

"I'm fine, sir. Thank you."

She went to the study to look for her checkbook, listening to hear if there were voices coming from the living room. She sat down at the desk and opened the drawer. That was when she first heard Tom talking softly, below the sounds of the television. He had such a hard time forming words, making the sounds with his mouth, that those who weren't used to listening closely often didn't understand him. Still, she was glad now that someone new was there to talk with her husband, and she allowed herself to linger over her checkbook.

Even before Regis Philbin, it seemed that they had run out of things to say. Already in their fifties when they married, everything had been wonderful getting to know one another and relearning how to live with another person, for a while, but after the first few years, they had been forced into the fight against Tom's disease that had robbed them of so many pleasures.

She could still hear Regis talking and wished she had turned off the volume, or the set altogether, before she had left them alone. She decided to go and turn off the set, but as she came into the living room, she stopped, remaining in the doorframe where they couldn't see her.

Adam was saying how he'd studied History in college, how he had gone to Spain for part of a summer, where a professor of his connected him with a two-week program in Madrid, after which he'd traveled around the country on a train pass. This seemed to excite Tom. He hadn't sat up as straight in a while and he seemed to make every effort to look at the boy, to see into his eyes. Elizabeth wondered if they'd talked to each other before.

"How did you like Barcelona?" Tom said.

The boy was quiet when Tom spoke, careful not to talk over him. He leaned down to see Tom's eyes, to bring his ear closer to Tom's mouth, and nodded when he understood.

"It was good," Adam said. "It's not my favorite city, but I love some things about it, especially the architecture by Gaudi."

"Spain must have changed," Tom said. "When I was there it was not a nice country. They stopped us in Figueras and we had to spend some time in prison before we could move on."

"You said it's changed?"

Tom spoke again, but this time his mumbling sounded worse. When he spoke, his lips didn't get as far as he wanted; they got in the way, cut him off. He had to just let words go, push them out with his neck, where most of his sounds were formed, and hope it made sense. Especially his "S's"—they all fell out flat, empty lisps.

"They put us in prison," Tom said. Even with everything, he really wanted to talk—she could see this—and he wouldn't settle for anything about the weather, anything common; he was trying to explain to Adam about a trip to Europe he'd taken some sixty years ago. "We were trying to drive an ambulance to Portugal and they held us up in Figueras," he mumbled.

"Prison?" Adam saw her and looked to her, as if for help. She tried to act as if she were just watching Regis—to keep the illusion that they were alone—but she couldn't help taking the remote off the coffee table and muting the TV. She sat down on the couch, between Adam and the TV.

"When I was nineteen," Tom said again, "I drove an ambulance through France and Spain to Portugal." She watched Tom, hoping to encourage Adam to keep listening, but noticed the way he stared at Tom's mouth when he spoke.

"To Portugal?" Adam asked. "From where?"

"From Paris, where I was living. When I was your age I studied there. I met people who volunteered in Portugal. They were driving an ambulance down. We would drive the ambulance in Portugal."

"What year was this?"

Tom stopped and made a noise in his throat, a little thing he did when he was thinking. "I think it was 1930's. Thirty-seven."

"Wow," Adam said. "That's wow. Like Hemingway times."

"But they stopped us in Figueras," Tom said. Adam made a face, and when he asked again what Tom had said, Tom repeated himself. "In Spain," he said, "they put us in prison. In Figueras."

"Prison," Adam said. "In 1937. In Figueras." Elizabeth could see how hard this was, wondered why Tom couldn't be satisfied with talking about the weather, something more simple: like sports, or a book even. Elizabeth checked the clock on the top of the piano: there was just over fifteen minutes left in Millionaire.

In a deep way, Elizabeth Richard had become tired with being the only one for Tom to talk to. Beyond just its sound, the game show was something she allowed herself because she was tired of acting as Tom's interpreter when he tried to talk about things that were beyond what he could communicate, tired of being the only one he talked to, and of Tom expecting her to always make the extra effort necessary to understand him. She knew he had no other choice, but still, she was tired. Now she watched as Adam continued to glance at her quizzically, but she pretended she wasn't there. She just wanted the two of them to go on talking. Maybe, she considered, if they did then Tom would learn something about how little he could communicate and how hard this was for her. Maybe he would realize not to start long conversations about sixty year-old subjects with their paper boy.

"Why would they put you in prison?" Adam asked.

Tom's head had begun to droop; he was facing his bowl again. "They said they had to check our papers. Then, when they came back, they took us to the jail. There was a British woman with us, and they let her go. She returned to France. But the others and I stayed."

Adam watched and nodded.

"Franco held the power then and he could have been suppressing our aid to Portugal. But we didn't know it." Tom's face strained when he spoke, then he dragged his bent hand across his face, wiping his mouth with the side of his first finger. The room became quiet. Outside, the winter wind blew hard against the house, and a branch scratched at a kitchen window.

As soon as Elizabeth noticed Adam watching the TV, she turned it off. He looked at her for a moment, maybe even got ready to say something, but then she turned to Tom. He appeared startled that she had done this, and he looked at her without speaking. He leaned back so that he could see her, so she could see his eyes. She saw nothing special in them, just Tom, her husband, as present and alive as he'd always been, his expression as normal as if he'd just finished his soup.

"Wait," Adam said, "But I'm still not sure why you were going to Portugal," and Tom started answering him again, nodding his head as he spoke. He told Adam about his studying poetry on a leave from Harvard in Paris for a year, and about

Franco and the Spanish Civil War, the Portuguese uninvolvement, and the types of people you could meet in those days, for whom peace was so important. He told Adam how the others had the ambulance, but that they needed a driver. "And, at the time," he said, "Peace seemed more important than poetry."

Adam had leaned closer to listen, bending down to Tom's face. His expression was one that Elizabeth Richard had not seen in some time: it was not the look of her husband's doctor, or that of the day-nurse who gave him his baths: Adam tilted his head as if to bring his ear closer to a precious sound, something he cared about hearing, and when he nodded it was a simple acknowledgement of one person understanding another.

She looked at the two of them and opened her mouth to speak, then shut it for fear of intruding. They looked so right, almost like two normal people chatting. "Tom's done some very interesting things over the years," she said, and then, surprised at the sound of her own voice, its loudness and clarity, she stopped. They each looked at her, as if they hadn't expected her to speak then, and she could hear the wind outside in the silence. She remembered how quiet their house could be. "I'm sorry," she said. "The two of you were talking."

Adam smiled at her. "It's some story he's telling. I've read about Paris in those days, but I never knew anyone who was there."

Elizabeth studied the boy: he was young and handsome, a strong college student who had lots of other places he could be. But he was here, listening to her husband. She touched his shoulder. "Let me show you something," she said. She led him to the piano in the front of the room. "Tom did this," she said, pointing to a green and yellow painting. "It's the last one he did before he lost the motor control in his hands."

"I hadn't known he was an artist."

"He used to paint," she said, "beautifully."

Tom remained hunched over his tray, looking down into the soup that would now be cold in its bowl. Some of his hair was sticking straight out from his head, and his lower lip worked itself under his upper, moving like a part on a machine. She watched him move his finger across his chin, just below his lip.

"That's a prison camp, right?" Adam said. "It's not Spain, is it?"

"It's a camp in Germany where Tom was for two years during World War II," she said.

In the painting, a block of men wearing blue-green coveralls stood handcuffed together outside of a building under a yellow sky, surrounded by black-clad guards. They filled the center of the canvas, holding themselves erect with slumped shoulders. There had always been something about the painting, the color of the sky or the prisoners' clothes, perhaps the way they held themselves, that was not altogether dark.

Adam studied the painting with wide eyes. "It's amazing," he said.

"It was a Nazi work camp," she said. "But Tom says it wasn't always bad. It wasn't a death camp. No one died there."

Despite its subject, the painting held beauty. Perhaps the

colors are what save it from being sad, she thought. The yellow of the sky held optimism and real hope: it wasn't falling on the captives, it was suspended above them, holding itself up like an attainable goal, a reassurance.

"Tom met other Americans there," she said. "Canadians, French, even British. The Germans worked them all hard, he says, but they weren't cruel."

Tom sat sideways in his chair, his head cocked to one side, watching them. His face was calmer, and his lip seemed still. He hunched over and forward, facing down, but he had moved the soup bowl onto the chair beside him.

"Why was he in Europe?" Adam asked.

"He went to Canada and joined the Canadian Army before the US involvement," she said. "He actually defected to fight for what he believed in."

"Peace was more important than poetry," Adam said. He reached toward the painting, as if to touch it, but stopped short. "I never knew anyone who could paint like this."

She heard Tom say, "That's enough about me now," though he'd become even harder to understand. When she turned to him, he motioned with his hand for them to return to the couch.

Adam looked at his watch. "I should get going," he said. He went over to Tom and thanked him, shaking the small twisted hand between both of his own. "Thanks for the stories," he said. "Spain is different now. The people are friendly."

Tom nodded. "I hope so."

Elizabeth followed Adam out of the living room and into

the front hall, where he stooped to put his boots on. As he did, she rushed back into the study and grabbed her checkbook. She tore off the check she'd written and took forty dollars out of her wallet, stuffed them both into a plain white envelope.

"Thanks for showing me that painting," Adam said, as she returned to the hall. She handed him the envelope and opened the door, pretending not to notice the way he looked at her legs again. When outside, he turned and thanked her, and she thanked him then closed the door. She watched him through the window as he folded the envelope, tucked it into the pocket of his jacket, and took out his package of cigarettes. He lit one and walked back to his car.

She locked the door then and turned off the porch light. The hall was dark. She crossed back to the living room, where Tom sat in his chair, his hands resting on the tray-table. She walked to the front of the room and looked at the painting one last time before turning off the lamp by the piano. She took Tom's bowl into the kitchen and washed it, then set it in the rack to dry. She considered sitting down in the kitchen, at the table by herself—where she usually collected her thoughts— but went back to the living room and Tom. When she sat down next to her husband and put her arm around him, she noticed his hair again and took the opportunity to smooth it down along the back of his skull, rubbing her hand over the curve of his back when she had done.

"Are you ready to go up?" she asked.

He nodded.

She took his arm and lifted him partly, waiting for his own legs to support him and do the rest of the job. As she helped him to stand, she reached into the hall for his walker and brought it around to stand next to him. He gripped the gray plastic handles intently, bowed over, and began his shuffle into the hall. She followed. When he had reached the bottom of the stairs, he turned and she helped him sit back into his lift-chair, the device they had had installed to carry him up to their second floor, and then she belted him in. When he nodded his readiness, she started the machine. It hummed and clicked as it carried him slowly up the stairs, on a diagonal against the wall where they had once had a banister. When it had clicked its way to the top, one movement at a time, he smiled down at her and she realized that she had just watched him, without moving, and that this was not something she usually did. At the top of the stairs he waited for her to come help him into his wheelchair. She shut off the rest of the downstairs lights and made sure the door was locked again before coming up.

"Daydreaming?" he asked, as she followed him up. She laughed and, bending down to lift him, wrapped his arms around her neck. She felt his breath against her face as she had when they were first married, dancing together at The Plaza on their wedding night. They had eloped, but done it in style. She remembered his crisp black tuxedo and the way his cummerbund stretched across his thin waist. He was a good dancer then and they had danced as if they wore slippers of air. She'd never felt so romantic.

Now she pulled him close to her and squeezed her arms around his back, pressing his face into her neck. His stubble scratched her cheek and she remembered that tomorrow she would have to shave him. But she could smell his old smell, the same him underneath the medications and the old clothes, and she liked that. "Ready?" she said.

"Yes."

She held her breath and lifted, his thin form pressing tight against her as she turned and then, bending at her knees, settled him down into his wheelchair. It always amazed her how light his body had become, that his limbs were so frail now. Though caring for him and lifting him had never been chores she'd expected, she had grown to enjoy the difference the work made in her arms, the methods of care that she'd learned from his doctors, the nurse.

"Thank you," he said. He was always grateful.

With the electric wheelchair, he moved himself into the bathroom, where she squeezed toothpaste onto his toothbrush. He picked it up himself and brushed his teeth. When he was done, he set it back on the edge of the sink and leaned forward to spit. She rinsed out the basin and handed him a glass of water. He drank some and spit into the basin again. She wet his washcloth for him with warm water, waiting until it got to be the right temperature before adding soap. He washed his face and around his neck, and then, after she unbuttoned his shirt, under his arms. Then, as he sat next to her, watching, she filled the sink and washed her own face. Early on, when they first started using the bathroom together, he had sometimes whistled, but now he could only manage a hum. Tonight it was Mahler's second symphony that he began as she washed her face and took down her hair.

When she had finished her ablutions, she wheeled him into the bedroom and folded back the blankets before helping him change into his nightclothes. Lifting him now, she felt his cheek against hers and the delicate vibration of his face from his humming, but she also felt her husband turn his face just slightly to kiss her. "Thank you," she said and when she settled him down onto the mattress, she made sure he was comfortable and fitted the blankets around him before she went around to her side, changed into her nightgown, turned off the lights, and climbed in.

In the darkness, she felt for Tom beneath the sheets with her hands as she slid over toward him. She found his hand and squeezed it lightly.

"Mahler," she whispered. "Mahler's second."

Still humming, Tom squeezed her hand in return. She felt his other hand take her wrist.

"Thank you for the accompaniment," she told him.

She took her husband in her arms then and, making sure he had enough room to breathe, she kissed him on the lips. She held his thin, weakened body, and felt his lungs fill part-way with air and then empty. She felt his heart beating steadily inside of him, a pounding organ inside his chest like anybody else's, and she felt an immeasurable joy spreading through her, knowing that the man she loved was still alive.

too early

Corinne rolls onto her side. This gives Adam the chance to
retract his arm from beneath her and cradle it to his chest. He is
glad to change the position of his shoulder. He's been awake for
a time, thinking, lying with his arm uncomfortable under her
neck. It is 4:37AM.

He holds both arms against his chest now, waiting for
sleep, though when it doesn't come he cuddles Corinne, kisses
the back of her neck. She rolls over to face him with her eyes
still closed, and traces her fingers across his chest.

"I can't sleep," he says.

"Then tell me a story." He has done this for her in the past,
and it has worked—for both of them. But tonight he has no
story to tell.

He asks her to roll back over and she does, putting her back
to him. He fits his knees behind hers and brings his top arm
around. She holds it, pulling his forearm to her chest, then lifts
her head for him to slide his other arm beneath it. Gently, he

slips his arm under her pillow, the angle of his shoulder changed just enough, and reaches around to his other arm, hugging her. Careful not to let her hair tickle his nose, he moves his head closer, close enough to rest his lips against her neck.

He can still feel the wall too close behind him, frigid and distinctly foreign, unnatural. She brings the inside of his wrist to her lips, and kisses it. "Are you OK?" she asks.

He tells her he will be all right.

She knows him as a writer, though he has not written in weeks. This she does not know. She asks him to tell her stories: always in bed, always late at night. The first few times he told her important stories, ones he had to tell. But now those are told; he has no more.

"Make me sleepy," she says.

"I can't, or I don't know if I can," he says. "I can't sleep either."

"What is it?"

"I'm not sure."

"What are you thinking?"

He doesn't know. His thoughts have drifted from one important-feeling idea to another. He's had this trouble before. "I've been awake," he says.

As she repositions her head on the pillow, her hair tickles his nose. His shoulder begins to shake again from this position, so he straightens his arm.

"Once," he begins, and then says, "I can tell you a small one, but it might not even be a story, really."

"It's OK," she says. "I want to hear it."

"I went to Washington D.C. with my dad once. I was

seven, maybe. Eight." He moves his legs closer to hers so that they are parallel, and sneaks his feet in between hers. She fits her head slightly higher on the pillow, moving her hair away from his face.

"I like D.C.," she says.

"I loved it. We saw the Smithsonian, Air and Space, the monument. I can't remember why we were down there, I think he had a conference or something.

"Maybe this isn't such a good story."

He waits, but she doesn't say anything. Then she kisses his hand. "It's OK," she says.

With his eyes closed, he tries to picture the vacation, to see the story he's trying to tell. "We stayed in a high-rise hotel," he says. "It was brick, I think, or dark concrete, and not so close to downtown. My father took me to a play I remember. I guess he tried to show me a good time."

He doesn't know what to do: whether he should make things up or tell what really happened. Neither will make much of a story. And they are new enough in their relationship that he still concerns himself with seeming perfect; some parts of himself he still tries to hide, such as his tendency to wake in the night wondering what could turn bad, or analyzing decisions he's made until they seem ready to dissolve.

"There's no story tonight," he says. "I'm sorry." His eyes closed, he listens to her breaths and tries to match them with his own. But her breaths are deeper and farther apart. In comparison, his seem shallow and quick. He feels her chest and shoulders expand with air then shrink.

Perhaps because she seems peaceful and might fall asleep,

leaving him alone, or because he is no different than anyone else —just pushing forward blindly in life, trying only his best to find what's right at any moment—he keeps telling what happened that night.

"We took a cab home after the play," he says. "A taxi. The cab had no meter—there's some system of zones in D.C. that tells how much a cab ride costs. My father just had a question because he didn't know which one we started in. But the driver didn't like that. He turned around in his seat and looked at us. I remember his eyes were tired, cold. He said, 'You think I don't give you right fare? You think I want rip you off?'" Adam doesn't remember the man's exact words, but these phrases come to him—whether from deep in his memory or from a desire to tell the story, he doesn't know.

"My father didn't know how the fare was decided, how they did it without a meter. The driver said, 'You look on map. Three zones! You look.' There was a map on the back of the front seat, below the glass. 'I don't understand,' my dad said. The cab driver hit the seat in front of us then threw his door open and got out of the car. He opened the door next to me and leaned inside, across my body, pointing to the map. I could smell him, this man who had sweat on his clothes, sweat and something else, something I couldn't place at the time but that I now know was curry. He tapped his finger against the plastic covering over the map, counting the places we had passed through. 'Three zones!' he said.

"My father had his wallet out already, finger-counting the bills. But then he put it back inside his coat. He opened the door on his side and got out of the cab, pulling me with him, away from the driver. 'I'm going to ask this doorman,' my father said. 'I just want to ask someone. I just want to know how this all works from one other person.' He saw the cabbie walking around to meet us at the front of the car and, raising his hands, said, 'It's not that I don't trust you.'

"The cabbie met us at the front of the car. 'I have no time for this,' he said. My father reached into his pocket and brought out the key to our room. He held it out to me and told me to go upstairs. He said to go watch TV. The room key was too big for my hand; I remember its big square top took up all of my palm. It was marked 325. 'Go!' my father said. The hotel doorman passed me as I started toward the hotel. 'Go!' my father said when I looked back. I could hear the cabbie yelling even as I moved inside the revolving doors.

"Inside I stopped to watch a young couple leave the hotel and start toward our cab. When they saw what was happening, they turned sharply and began walking away. The driver yelled after them. Then he said something to my father, pointing at the couple. At that point my father looked around. He saw where I was and our eyes locked. 'Go!' he yelled again, loud enough I could hear it through the glass. I ran to the elevators and reached up to push the button. A lady in a fur walked up and smiled at me but she didn't say anything. She got onto my elevator and stayed on after I got off. I ran down the hall of the third floor to 325, my feet clopping on the hotel carpet, and opened the door and ran straight to the windows."

He shifts slightly in the bed, edging away from the cold wall, closer toward her. "Corinne?"

"I'm here," she says. "Still listening." She lifts his hand from her chest, kisses it. "Keep going," she says.

"Our room was on the front of the hotel, the driveway side. I climbed up on the radiator and put my hands against the glass, but all I could see was a part of the cab, not my father. A big concrete overhang, the kind to guard our entrance from rain, blocked my view. It was covered with a layer of pebbles like a driveway. The window was cold against my hands, I remember, and outside it was dark and the sky was black and without any stars. Across the street from our hotel was a park with some grass.

"I want to say I remember seeing the White House in the skyline, or some capitol building, the lights on a dome in the night, but I don't know if that's true, or even possible.

"I stayed against the glass, looking out into the night, wanting to see the cab leave. I watched a man walk down the sidewalk on the other side of the road from me. He fought against the cold, leaning into the wind with his hands in his pockets. For some reason I wanted him to see me; I wanted him to look up and see me so I could wave and he would know everything was all right. But he never looked up, just walked with his face toward the ground. Finally the cab drove off, puffs of condensation trailing from its tailpipe. I got down fast and put the TV on then, and waited on the edge of the bed for my dad."

He feels too warm in the bed suddenly, as if heat has built up through the night, and he would like to take away their blankets and lie in the air. Without disturbing her, he slips one leg out from under the covers. "Can we roll this way?" he says, taking her arm and hinting it toward the wall. His shoulder is shaking again and his side is tired. "Is it OK to switch over for a while?" He wants also to be spooned, to feel her arms around him, even though her body is small. Willingly, obligingly, she moves.

On his left side now, he touches the wall in front of him

with the tips of his fingers, his hand a spider on the wall. He feels its tiny bumps and craters, but then she is kissing his neck and he closes his eyes. She slides her arm under his, close to his body. He puts his hand on hers.

"Is this OK for you?" he asks.

She hums a simple noise that means yes, squeezes him tight around his chest. "What happens in the story?"

He closes his eyes, feeling her breathing behind him, the small movements of their bodies. The image of his father coming through the door of the hotel room stands in his mind. He sees the dark blue handkerchief his father held to his brow, the blood in a line down his cheek. This is the part he has not wanted to tell, the part that matters. Adam pushes himself up onto his elbows.

"What's the matter?" she asks.

"He got punched—my dad. When he came in he was bleeding from over his eye. The cabbie had hit him.

"My father," he says.

He lies back down beside her, his hands by his sides. She has retreated her arm and he wants it now, but doesn't ask, can't. In telling this, he has passed what he knew was right to say. Now he is open to her evaluation. He closes his eyes.

"Adam?" she says. When he doesn't answer, she reaches across his body for his hand and pulls it toward her. She tugs at him, on his side, rolling him over, and sets his arm behind her back. Again she slides her arm under his and this time squeezes him more tightly against her. Though he feels like dead weight in her arms, he allows himself to be moved, held.

"The cabbie punched him," he says. "My father told me the guy lost his temper, grabbed at his sleeve. Then, when my dad jerked away, the guy hit him. Just cocked and swung. Then the doorman stepped in.

"I remember my dad had a handkerchief pressed up against his face to stop the blood. He went into the bathroom, but I could see him through the open door. I stood outside, watching as he washed the blood from his face with a washcloth. I watched him run water into the sink and cup his hands in it, bring water up to his face. Blood ran over his hands and down his wrist. He wet the handkerchief and held it against his temple."

• • •

After he hasn't said anything for a while, she asks if that is all.

She turns around to face him and now he can see her clearly in the morning light. Somewhere the sun has begun to rise. People will be starting their days.

"That was the story," he says. "The hotel doorman broke up the fight, really it was only that one punch, not a fight so much. That's the whole thing."

She examines his face, and then lays her forehead against his chest. His hand has found her hip, but he feels it shouldn't have. Her leg feels too hot, her skin smooth, like the wall. He lifts his hand away, rests it on his side.

"I'm sorry I told you that story," he says.

In the silence he can hear a humming from far off, a distant rumble that he's heard at night before when he can't sleep, when he's alone. It has to be the highway, he knows, though that's over a mile away. He hasn't heard it since he met her.

too early

"Do you hear that sound?" he asks. "It's the highway, I think. Must be the trucks going across at night."

"I hear a bird," she says. "I hear what you're saying, but a bird too. I guess it's morning."

"We'll be tired today."

"Do you hear that dog?" She brings her hand away from his back and he feels her fingers tickle his side then move along his chest, up to his neck and then the side of his face.

He hears the clear, distinct barking of the neighbor's dog. It barks at anything that comes near. "I hear it barking," he says. He touches her shoulder gently, at first, then cups his palm over it. He can feel the strong bone under her skin. He slides over, as close to her as he can come, his legs intertwined with hers. He kisses her.

"I'm sorry I kept you from sleeping," he says.

"You don't have to apologize."

"I am though."

He feels small, as a scared boy who is lucky to have someone with him feels, and remembers begging his father not to leave the edge of his bed at bedtime when he was a boy. He isn't sure what to say now, or what to do, and worries that what he's already done might scare Corinne away. If he can just stay quiet, he hopes, this feeling will pass. Perhaps she will soon forget it all and believe that he is strong enough to sleep through the night.

"I wake up sometimes in the mornings," he says. "Like this. When it's too early to get up. I just wake up and think and I can't stop. I wish I could sleep."

He closes his mouth, fights off the urge to say more. He waits for what will happen, counting his breaths. If he can wait long enough, he might fall asleep, he thinks. His arm is draped awkwardly over her. He can feel the pains in his stomach for breakfast, but ignores them. There is a tingling in his legs, above his knees.

Corinne rolls over so her back is against his chest and cradles his arm in hers. "Put your other arm under my head," she tells him. He puts his arm under her neck again and his shoulder feels tender, but he doesn't move it. With his top hand, he touches along the slope of her side and explores the space below her belly-button: the slight pucker around her middle. They bend their knees. Her breasts are small, like half-peaches, but her nipples are full, round. He touches them and she taps his hand, weaves her fingers between his. Her hand feels rough and dry. Her fingernails are cut short, like a man's. With his thumb, he feels the place on her finger where the nail sinks in at the middle as if it's been struck with a hammer, but he knows it grows like this—she has told him. He runs the tip of his finger along the crease.

"That's my funny thumb," she says.

He wants to tell her he's sorry for it, for her thin arms and dry hands. He wants to apologize for the time she lost her job and how his legs are bowed and because his chest isn't muscular and his stomach is too round.

"I wake up early sometimes," he says.

She holds his hand in hers and brings it up to her mouth. A gentle stream of breath tickles the inside of his wrist. Then she kisses his palm. "It's OK," she tells him. "I don't mind."

Michigan

"Michigan," she said, softly. My grandmother. She held my hand with her limp post-stroke fingers and looked up into the T-shirt I wore. "Michigan," she read, again.

"Grandma, I'm here. It's Adam." I squeezed her hand.

"Mi-chi-gan." She read slowly, as if exploring the yellow letters on my blue shirt, hunting for their meaning, and of course there was none, just an old T-shirt I'd pulled from a drawer. Her eyes roamed in their sockets, floated like floating candles. She would not meet my eyes, only stared up at my shirt as if trying to solve a puzzle.

"Grandma," I said.

She rolled back to the center of her pillow and looked straight up at the ceiling.

"I'm here now, Grandma."

Her wrinkled lips hung over her small gums. Without her dentures, her face looked narrow, thin, her mouth almost beaklike. She had thrown up all over her clothes last night and lost her dentures while she lay on the floor of her bathroom, kicking for help until morning, when one of the aids came to find her after she missed breakfast.

I had never seen her without her teeth. A dark liver spot had taken over the right side of her upper lip.

"What happened, Grandma? Where are Dianne and Uncle Al?"

She looked up to the TV set, though it was off. "Five ABC, Seven CBS," she read from the sign on its front. "Four NBC," she said.

I sat down in the chair beside her bed, an orange cushioned number that slowly released air from its plastic cushion until it had settled under me. "That's what the TV says," I said. "Those are the channels."

"Seven CBS," she said.

I looked around the bright room. A fresh-made bed by the window had a blue sheet and blanket identical to my grandmother's, turned down and folded back to perfection. The large window let in mid-afternoon, late-May sun. I stood and walked to the TV, reached up to where it was fastened high on the wall and touched the front of it, ran my fingers over the raised lettering of the sign she'd read, and turned back toward her. She saw me, I believe, and I waved. "Hi, Grandma," I said.

She did not move or respond; her hands remained by her sides.

I went back and sat next to her, lowered my hand then to touch hers as it lay on the covers. I brushed along her loose knuckles and the plane of soft, spotted skin below where a tube ran into her arm. She turned to look up at me and for a moment her eyes scanned my face before they fell back to the blue and yellow of my shirt-front. "Mi-chi-gan," she said again, softly.

"Grandma, it's just a shirt," I said. "Michigan basketball. It's a college team."

Her head rocked back onto her pillow. She looked straight up, her lips moving slightly, her silver hair disheveled, as if she were searching for something above her, something to help her understand what was going on. I wanted to explain that I was her grandson come to visit before attempting to drive across the country in a van purchased with a few other friends. I wanted to tell her that this was the last time I would see her in a while, or have her ask me to stay, ask me to abandon my adventurous summer and stay here to help her. Ultimately, though I didn't know it at the time, this was the last time I would see her alive.

I wanted to say so much more to her, to help her and do something, but there were only five more minutes of visiting hours and I didn't know what else to do.

I held her hand. Her face looked thin on the light blue pillow. I told her it was just a T-shirt. I told her I was her grandson and that I loved her.

cherry tree

The weeping cherry in front of our house has bloomed its white blossoms, meaning spring has come. Early spring in Cambridge, which means rain and cold interspersed with days of warmth and sun. Unfortunately, after the first April days of sun, the cherry always blooms small white petals all over its hanging branches, a huge cloud of white in our yard, the most beautiful sight on our block for the year. And then in the next weeks the weather turns cold again. This happens every year, and I invariably wish the tree had waited to release its blossoms, to turn itself white with flowers, until after the winds and rain. If it bloomed in May, I reason, the petals would stay on its tentacles longer, instead of blowing onto the ground and sliding down the gutters in running streams of rain down the hill. But each year, the tree blossoms early, and I remind myself that Spring is here, even in the cold and the rain. For a few wonderful days, your house is surrounded by flowers.

"Don't ever break your own heart," my mother tells me. She sits across from me in a booth at the big Korean-sushi restaurant near her house, about a five-minute walk from my dad's, the big house at the top of the hill, the one with the tree in the front yard. I'm living with him now, stay there while I look for a job. I have finished college, graduated with honors, moved to New York City to start a job, left it, lived on savings and worked on a novel, and moved home. In all truth, the house belongs to my stepmother, my father's second wife, who lives with us as well. She bought it some years ago with her first husband, who has since gone crazy, sent himself to Northern Maine, and is no longer around. But this is the house they raised their kids in, and now she lives there with another man, and his son—me.

"Are you listening?" my mother says. She is drunk on sake and beer, not something that happens often, but from time to time. When she gets this way, my mother tells stories. Tonight she will tell me about my father and how she left him, how she thought it was the right thing to do, had it all figured out. "I knew I could change and it would make my life better," she'll say. Perhaps we are both melancholy from the rain outside, the steady downpour that I can see making dime-sized stars in circles on the skylight just a few feet above my head, set against the still-light gray sky. Perhaps we have both had too much to drink, an event that has happened more than a few times since I have moved home.

"But you should never leave love," she says.

"I know, Mom."

"Whatever you're thinking in your head is ideas. You lose love and it's a part of you; all the other plans you had will change." She shakes her head. "You know this," she says, "Because you're like me. You can feel it."

"I know, Mom," I say. I could tell her that I do know what she means, exactly, but she wouldn't believe me; I could tell her the stories about how I've learned it for myself—that you let love go, you leave it, it's like taking a piece of yourself away that doesn't come back and while it's gone it's like you're somebody else. I could tell her I know how when you're alone it's all different and nothing you wanted to do will work like you'd planned it; how you don't want to do anything but sleep and wait for the hurt to leave, but I don't. I don't tell her any of it that I know, now, after what happened with Sarah.

She shakes her head again and taps her sake shot glass against the table for me to fill it up again, which I do. I want to say something to her, something else to keep a conversation going, to keep her from telling me about my dad, but I've run out of relatives to ask after and things that have happened to tell.

The rain seems to be letting up outside and on the skylight. It means I won't get wetter walking home and that maybe I'll be able to excuse myself soon, get back to my room and my thoughts.

I want to tell her about my second year in college, the year that Amy started hanging around and I got to know her, the year I called Sarah one week before my birthday and told her to cancel her plane ticket, not to come for the weekend and visit, because I thought it was the right thing to do.

In Chicago I had three more years of college, on one hand, and a beautiful girl, Amy, who I kept finding myself alone with, whose arm touched my arm at the movies, and who once picked blades of grass off my elbow when we were laying on the grass at a poetry reading in the middle of the quad.

At home, in Boston, Sarah went to Emerson and called me every night. She didn't fear spending money on phone bills, or flying out to visit, just wanted us. And I loved her. She was beautiful, smart, and funny. My friends liked her and she liked my friends. I had my doubts whether we could stay together through three years of school with half the country between us, something else worried me about the fact she wasn't Jewish. Her family was so different from mine. A part of me doubted and a part of me couldn't believe that a girl as beautiful as Amy existed in my life. When I told my friends that I had to give Amy the truth about Sarah, and tell her the line about "Let's be friends," they nodded, but they didn't know: they thought I could do it.

"We need to talk," I said to Sarah, on the phone.

"About plans for your birthday?"

"Partly about that," I said.

• • •

I told her because I could talk to her, tell her how I felt, and didn't realize that that was one part of love. Part of the fix of this whole thing, I understand now, is that the one you love is the one you can talk to, reason with, explain your conflicted feelings to. What I didn't know is that that talk can bring you closer, change how you can exist without that person, dig you into a well that doesn't go away in a few days or weeks, changes how you act around the rest of the people in your life and how much fun you are, how much people like you. By the time I got off the phone I had broken Sarah's heart and my own.

After that, I tried to duck Amy for a while. I still wanted to be with her, but I couldn't be around her when I was still thinking about Sarah. We didn't laugh together and for my birthday I had dinner with some other friends. That was how it would go, how it went and never really got fixed right. I kissed Amy a few times, hollow, hopeful kisses that were my way of expressing that I wanted to be with her, that I hoped she would still be with me when I became myself again, when my heart mended. But in the weeks that followed, the kisses became more hollow and then became stolen, something that I had to spring on Amy when she didn't expect it, a small thing without feeling that I held to as my last claim to what was only an idea: the thought that we could be together.

But I don't say any of this to my mother. She knows the same lesson, I gather, from what she went through with my dad. The tall, thin waitress in the white shirt leaves our bill at the edge of the table in a small leatherette case and my mom looks at it. She'll pay tonight, as she always does, whether I want to or not. She upends the small sake jug over my thimble-shot glass and dribbles out the rest of our bottle. It has gone cold some time ago, but I drink it, knocking back what's left in one gasp.

"I'm sorry," she says. "We could've ordered another bottle." My mother picks up the check and looks at it, slides a credit card into the small pocket that keeps it, lets half of it stick out of the case for the waitress to see we're ready to go.

Huesca

"Ta git it inta reverse ya've gut ta pull the wee ring aroond it," the man at the Budget Rent-A-Car in Barcelona told them, explaining how they could get the little Renault into reverse. "Ya hafta joost pull up on the wee ring," he said.

"OK," the boy said. He had his mind full of how to get out of Barcelona, how they'd head up toward San Sebastian, and what the exchange rates meant this car was costing them for the week, and now on top of that, he was getting a lecture in deep Scottish brogue on how to get the car into reverse. It was enough, too much, just perfect. Here he was, fighting to understand and speak Spanish, and he could hardly understand this guy's *English*.

"I'm liftin the *wee* ring," the boy said, when they'd gotten into the car and were ready to pull out into traffic on Diagonal. She laughed. Her own accent was a variation of British that sounded slower than the average, but she was really from Germany. He'd often doubted whether anyone'd be able to place her voice to a country—he'd thought she was Scandinavian when he first met her—and though his friends at home liked her accent, they didn't know enough about Europe to expect she'd be German.

She had the map out in front of her and was trying to piece together how they'd get to the Nacional. "We want to quickly take a left here at the next street and then turn around," she advised him. He backed the car out and pulled into midafternoon, screaming Barcelona traffic.

• • •

The scooter drivers in Barcelona managed to smoke while they rode around the city, swerving in and out of cars, she noticed as they passed through yet another neighborhood that was supposed to lead them to the outside of town.

"There's a sign," he said. "Look, it's pointing to that part of the rotary. We can just continue around like this, and…." He pointed to and she saw the sign that said N-33 San Sebastian, and she relaxed as they headed down yet another major thoroughfare, passing wonderful-looking Spanish cafés, bread stores, and tapas bars.

"This is such an amazing city," she told him, thinking of the day before. It'd been a Sunday and the stores were closed, but they'd managed to find an open pharmacy to sell them sunscreen and sitting at the cafés was even nicer with the streets mostly empty. He'd showed her some Gaudi architecture and taken her to a museum in an apartment building. There they'd taken pictures of each other on the roof, next to the incredible moldings and statuesque chimneys. The weather was beautiful. In the gift shop of the museum, he'd bought her a necklace that was one of the most beautiful things she'd ever seen: it wrapped around itself and shrunk up on her neck looking crinkled, punctuated with light blue baubles; it was exquisite. The woman who'd sold it to them, yet another Spanish woman more gorgeous than you could imagine, had showed her how it could be worn as a long necklace, or as a choker, or as a medium-length. Today she wore it as a choker. It was the first really nice thing he had ever bought her.

"That's something," he said, pointing to a really big sculpture of what looked like a globe. "I don't know what it is, but it's something."

"Maybe we should take the Autopista," she said. "It looks like it'll be faster than the Nacional."

"No," he said. "They go right side-by-side. Look at it on the map. The Nacional's better, too, because it doesn't cost any money. That Autopista's for suckers, I think."

"We can try the Nacional, but it looks like it'll take longer. It also seems to pass through a lot more towns."

Coming out of the city, they ended up on the Autopista without having any choice and he slashed the Renault in between cars, getting to the outside lane and going over 120kmh on the huge, four-lane, divided elevated highway. "Where's the Nacional?" he said. "This is the Autopista."

"There should be a turnoff soon to get onto the N-33."

"Can you do me a favor and see if you can find the CD player?" he asked.

She knew where it was: in the bottom of her backpack, behind his seat, on the floor of the car. Going as fast as they were made it harder, but she angled herself back to the bag and pulled it up into the front. His aversion to the Autopista was odd, she considered, since they were on vacation and the day before he'd been absolutely lovely. Not only had he bought her the necklace, but they'd gone to one of the nicest restaurants she'd ever been to and he hadn't complained once. But now he was worried about the tolls on the Autopista.

"What CD's do you have there?" he asked.

He chose the Charlie Parker Favorites and lit a cigarette as they got off onto the Nacional, a two-lane, two-direction *road* that passed right along the ground in the arid country region. Cars sped past them going the other way and trucks loomed ahead as he throttled the small stick shift up to fifth gear.

"Yeah," he said, as he jumped out into the opposite lane and made an end-run around a truck. "This is *European driving!*" They were going unbelievably fast along the small road, and she could feel the rush of the wind as they got around the truck and slid back into their lane not fifty feet away from an oncoming car. He hooted and hit his hand on the steering wheel. "This's what I'm talking about! *Euro*pean Driving!"

She hadn't even known him to smoke cigarettes in the past, but now that they "were on vacation" (as he put it), he said he was entitled. This was part of the speech he'd given her that morning when they got lost looking for a metro to take them to the Budget Rent-A-Car. Other parts of the speech included "process-oriented travel," which he explained to mean that they should enjoy how they got places, not just where they arrived. Hence the Nacional and this screaming blast through the farmland.

Twenty minutes later, they still had the windows down and he couldn't get around a truck and the two cars that trailed it. They'd slowed to 80kmh and they were passing farms in the distance; the close terrain was all empty, rolling hills. Charlie Parker still blew faster than she would have liked, driving tempos as fast as their car had previously been going.

"This is beautiful," she said.

"Yeah, you've got to love how old everything is over here. These hills haven't changed forever, that's not so big, but the buildings you see, those have been around for centuries. I love to see the old-style buildings."

"Where I'm from we have the same: buildings as old as these."

"What's the deal with this truck though? We can't get by it."

"It's nice just driving though."

"But I'm talking European Driving! Let's get around this thing!" With a rush of air, he jumped into the oncoming lane and then fell back to allow a passing car. He jumped out again and this time got around both cars; he squeezed in behind the truck as a passing car came at them. "Ready?" he said.

This business was starting to make her crazy, but she hung on to the handle above her door and *held on* as he jumped out, shifted down, and ran around the truck and back into their lane just before they started into another turn. He lit another cigarette.

The first town they came to had an old castle above the Nacional, up on a hill. He pointed to it and she tried to find something about it in their guidebook, but they didn't stop or get off the road. The longest they stopped was when they came to a red light in the center of town, and here he remarked that it looked like this place actually had people in it that lived their lives. She wasn't sure what he meant by this, but left it alone.

As the afternoon went on, the weather became incredibly hot. Having left the city and the coast, they were making their way through the rolling hills and into the mountains of Catalonia where the air was more humid because clouds got caught up in the hills.

Though he complained about the gas it'd take and the power it could draw from the engine, they put the air conditioner on when they got back on the road again and she got him to change the CD to something more relaxing. Now they rolled through the countryside more peacefully, and even when he did his end-runs around the trucks, it didn't bother her as much because the wind didn't alarm her and she could actually put it out of her mind that they were facing the oncoming traffic for moments at a time; she closed her eyes when she saw the cars rushing toward her and held to the handle above her head.

"Is this how they drive on the Autobahn?" he asked.

"No," she said. "It most certainly is not."

• • •

After several hours of the Nacional, he admitted he was ready for her to take over the driving. She was frazzled, too, and more than a bit tired, but she consented, mostly because she wanted to pull her share and didn't want to let him down. When she got behind the wheel, he put on his Charlie Parker CD again. "To get you in the mood," he said.

As soon as she began, he coached her about when to pass,

though from where he sat she doubted that he could see the oncoming lane; she wasn't fast enough for him. "You got to get around this one," he told her, pointing to a big white truck in front of them. "This thing's going to kill our time."

She tried to dart into the oncoming lane as he had, but every time she did there seemed to be a car coming too close for her to make her end-run.

"You could have had it that time," he assured her. After an attempt where she was certain the white car coming toward them had flashed its lights in warning, he said, "That one was yours without a doubt. You *had* that one." When the white car had passed, "OK. Now let's get ready and take a look." She poked into the oncoming lane just enough to see there were no cars coming. "You're OK," he said. "Go! Go! Go!"

She kept going: pushing the pedal down, she extended herself further into the oncoming lane and started to pass the truck. She had it up to 110kmh, then 120, then 130. When she got to the cab of the truck, she thought he sped up—the idea of hitting the brakes and going back to her old position behind him crossed her mind—and she pushed the pedal down harder to get by him.

"*Euro*pean Driving!" the boy in the seat next to her very nearly screamed.

Up ahead a green minivan came around a turn in her lane, not more than 200 feet off. "Oooh!" she said, pressing the gas down and checking to see if she could see the front of the truck in her side mirror. "Aaah!" She wanted to close her eyes, get it all over with, and stop this—her heart was racing and she could see her knuckles gripped too tightly on the wheel—and the green van was coming.

"*Euro*pean—"

"Shut up!" she yelled. "Shut up! Shut up! Shut up! Shut up!" She jumped the Renault back into the right-side lane and kept the needle rising past 140kmh to get the truck as far away from her as possible. She wanted to apologize to the green minivan as it sped past, but before she completed the thought it was gone.

"Turn this off!" she said then; though its knobs were still foreign to her, she clicked off the radio on her first try. "Stop it! We've got to calm this down. Stop it! I don't like this!"

"You mean you don't love the adrenaline, the—"

"No," she said. "No and no. This isn't fun. It makes me crazy out here in the heat and with the wind and passing these big cars on these little roads."

"It's crazy," he said. "But that's the fun of it. That's all the fun. Look, see this truck here?" Already they were coming up on another, a big grain truck with long mudflaps.

"Stop it! Stop it! Stop it! Stop it!" She came up behind the truck and held her speed.

"We're not passing—"

"Shhh," she said. "I'm going as fast as I want to."

"You don't like the *Euro*pean driving?"

"No. I don't like it. I want to relax and stop this craziness. It's too much for me. The next town we come to, that's going to be the one where we stop, and in the morning we look for the Autopista and get onto that." A small white car pulled around them and sped on. "Enough of this!"

• • •

The next town they came to was called Huesca. There were still a few hours to sundown, but he had never seen her go into such an outburst and he was willing to concede this battle to her—they were on a vacation and deserved a rest. The crowded streets frazzled her to the point where she pulled over and asked him to park the car. "We need to find a hotel and just check in and relax," she told him. "You park the car and I'm going to find something for us in the guidebook."

Driving the narrow streets was not a problem for him; he found a parking space on the first street he drove and pulled in. "How do the hotels look?" he asked.

"They look affordable," she said. "There are three hotels that look worth checking. I even think I can find them."

"It's a small town. How hard can it be?"

The summer air was still hot when they got out of the car. Spoiled by the air conditioning, he was reluctant to take their bags with them on their first excursion into the city and he left them, knowing he might regret it later. Though it was after 5pm, the streets were busy with pedestrians. The shops were still open: a shoe store, what looked like an underwear store, a store that sold hats; finally he saw a panaderia with long fresh-looking breads and a café that looked like it served tapas and beer. He thought he might have a chance of finding churros and chocolate in a town like this, items that had graced his ninth-grade Spanish textbook and intrigued him ever since. They followed the main street into the town center.

"This street is supposed to come into Calle Ainsa and then we take that," she said, consulting the map in the guidebook.

He hated to be the American tourists with the big guidebook, but that was what they were—even if she wasn't

American. None of the villagers seemed to notice it here though, as if they weren't used to having visitors. He felt as invisible as he would in any American city, or even more so, given what it was like to travel in some parts of the Northwest.

They came into a large plaza where the second stories of the buildings stretched out over the sidewalks to the road and cafés lined the streets. Each of them had tables set up under the overhang: rows of metal chairs and collapsible tables filled the plaza with lounging after-siesta Spaniards enjoying cigarettes and beer.

"This looks like a pretty good place to hang out," he said.

"Sure. As soon as we find our hotel."

After the plaza they came to Ainsa, which led to a pedestrian thoroughfare. They followed one corridor to another and came to the street that was to have the hotel. At the number listed in the guidebook, the hotel appeared to occupy the second floor. They buzzed up and were told to come in. The building wasn't air conditioned but it had an elevator that took them up to the lobby of the pension, which was as cool as they could ask for.

"Ask them what the rooms cost," she said, not speaking any Spanish herself.

He inquired and found that a room for the two of them came to just under sixty dollars. "Fine," she said. "Isn't that fine?"

It did seem good; not too long ago they'd spent over a hundred dollars for a room together in New York City when they went to visit some friends. Plus, this room had a bathroom; they were ready to relax, shower, and lay down; and the place was close to the plaza with the tables.

"We'll take it," he said, forgetting himself and using English. He finished the negotiations in Spanish.

The room was small but clean, with a balcony that overlooked the pedestrian alley and a small bathroom with a shower. The landlady gave them an old skeleton key to open and close the lock on the door and showed them where the light was in the hall. She said the lobby would be open all night and that she could recommend a restaurant for them to try.

"This is good enough," he said, flopping down on the bed. He hadn't realized how tired he was, but when he got his shoes off and she mentioned going back to get the bags, he realized that he was exhausted. Still, they found their way back to the car quickly, using a map from the hotel they saw a much easier route, and collected only enough of their luggage for one night. They consolidated it all into her bag and were able to leave the bulk of their things in the car. She was careful to take her valuables with them, though, and especially careful to make sure that she had the necklace he'd bought her.

They turned the air conditioner up full blast in the room and he looked out the balcony doors to the street below them. "You can have the first shower," she told him.

"OK if I wait a minute? I'm just going to smoke one and then I'll go." She didn't answer. "Is that cool?" he asked.

He looked in and saw her lying on the bed with her eyes closed in front of the A/C. She had her skirt pulled up to her above her knees and he could see where the soft blond hairs started above the part that she shaved. She looked like she wouldn't mind resting a minute, so he went out onto the balcony and had a cigarette.

After taking his shower, he woke her up and told her it was her turn. "I can meet you at one of those tables by where those cafés were, if that's all right?" he said. She nodded. "Do you remember how to get back there?"

"Mmmm," she said. "I can find it."

She was slowly getting up and collecting some clothes out of her bag when he closed the door and went out.

He found his way back to the café area without too much trouble and took one of the tables in the back row, separated from the street by a row of tables and a walkway for people. He felt glad that he was on vacation, glad to be tapping out a cigarette and especially for letting himself get away with smoking like this—he'd quit a year ago, but now he reasoned that he was on vacation—and so tired from the drive and the heat, more ready to have a beer than he'd been in as long as he could remember. Plus, she'd brought along a copy of the *New Yorker* Summer Fiction Issue, and he was glad to have that for company. That, and a bottle of beer, was more than all he needed.

When the little waiter came around wearing his black vest and bow tie, he was all smiles and asked the young man in Spanish what he'd like from the bar. "Cerveza," the young man said.

"Vaso?"

"Sí." The young man shrugged, not caring whether he got a glass with his beer or not.

After the waiter left, he lit a cigarette. He'd wanted to wait for the beer to come, but he didn't and that wasn't something he'd worry about. Perhaps he'd get some olives to suck on if he could remember how to say it in Spanish. He looked around and noticed that the women weren't as impressive here as those in Barcelona (but which were?) and that most of the people at the café were considerably older than him. There was a piece by Tobias Wolff in his magazine and he figured that'd be worth reading: he turned to the page, but continued to look around at the other tables.

Across from him, at the closest occupied table, were two men drinking beer out of frosted, frozen glasses. Hot as it was, the young man couldn't think of anything that sounded better than that. He stared at the glasses in awe, thinking about how cool a cold beer would taste right now and how much colder it could get with a frozen glass, how much better that would feel.

When the waiter came to drop off his beer, the young man asked him for a "glass cold" please and the man smiled knowingly and pointed at the next table. The boy nodded and smiled. It was not long before the small waiter brought back the frozen glass. When the young man touched it, he left fingerprints in the frost. He tilted it to the side and poured his beer in carefully, and took his first sip: it was the coldest, more earned-feeling beer he thought he'd ever had. Ice chips floated into his mouth. He practically wanted to gasp "Aaah" after his first pull, but resisted and lit a new cigarette, noticing that his previous had burned out on its own.

He poured the glass full again and sipped the beer as if it were some exquisite prize he'd won for traveling so far and coming to such an out-of-the-way town. It was a beautiful thing, this café: couples and business partners (or so he imagined) talked incessantly at tables around him and others lounged quietly over cigarettes as fancy cars pulled by slowly, waving at the drinkers and occasionally honking a horn in greeting. The people around him were dressed nicely, smartly, as the Spanish will do, and he felt glad to be wearing clean pants and a new linen shirt he'd picked up that morning in Barcelona.

He took a drag on his cigarette, looked down at his magazine to start reading, and had to admit that it could sometimes feel great to be alive.

• • •

She finished showering and applied the lotion to all parts of her body—this was something she did every day, but today it took on a special meaning, as if she savored the touch of her own hands more than usual, was extra conscious of the softness of her skin in the cool air conditioning of the hotel room.

"Huesca," she said out loud. It was good to just stop, really, she felt, but so far everything about the little town had been fine, wonderful even. Everything was fantastic, by comparison, after bombing on the hot little roads all afternoon in their car. She did not resent him for choosing the Nacional, but she had to admit that everything felt much, much better by comparison after such an awful experience. She moved to the balcony and looked down onto the street below. Spaniards walked back and forth carrying bread for their families, and sausages, vegetables, paper bags of things she couldn't see. It would be hot out there, but she looked forward to seeing him again, being with him in the café, and getting something to eat at a tapas bar if they could find a good one. She put on her backless halter top and the necklace he'd bought her at the Gaudi Museum in Barcelona.

On her way out, she asked the woman who ran the hotel if she could recommend a good restaurant for tapas. The woman didn't understand her English, but when the girl made a motion for food going into her mouth, the woman pointed to a stack of cards on a table. She went over to them and picked one out: El café Henri.

Outside it was still hot in the streets, but the sun was getting close to when it might set, and she felt comfortable in clean pants and her backless top. She had polished her toenails and put on eyeliner before coming outside, and she was glad it was cool enough that she wouldn't have to worry about sweating. She was glad for that.

It wasn't hard to trace her way back to the plaza of tables where she knew she would find him. He was bent over the magazine, reading intently, a glass of beer in his hand.

"Don't you look civilized?" she said, approaching. He got up and offered her a chair. "What's this?"

"Would you care to sit down, madame?"

"Who *are* you?"

"Please," he said. They both sat down. "It's so nice here. I've just been reading and—get this! You won't believe it, but they'll bring you a beer and a frozen glass to drink it from here. It's the best thing that's ever happened to me."

She couldn't help but laugh along with his enthusiasm and found it refreshing after all the times he'd been glum or less-than-ecstatic when she'd been around him.

"Do you know that I've been waiting for you?" he said. "Did you know that? There's a time when two people need some time apart on a trip like this, I'm sure you understand, but it's nice to miss someone, too. And what I'm saying is that I missed you, my dear. Did you have any trouble finding me?"

"Not at all," she said, playing along.

The waiter came over to them and interrupted, "Perdón?"

"Dos cervesas con vasos frios," the young man said.

"Bien."

She liked that he could speak Spanish, that they could get by here because of him, and the feeling of having things done for her. This was new to her, and she considered it something that she'd like to see more often. "I love our vacation," she told him.

The pack of cigarettes was on the table and she noticed him touching the cardboard. He picked up the box and then put it back down.

"Smoke if you want to," she said.

"Yes, well. No, the thing is I'd rather wait for our beer to come before I have another." He drained off what was left in his glass.

"You're so different on vacation," she said. "This is first time I think I've seen you relaxed."

"It might just be. In *fact* you may never see me as relaxed as this ever again. Or you might."

"I hope so."

The waiter returned with their order and set the glasses down, then poured them half-full of beer—hers first, and then his. He slid a small metal tray down onto the edge of the table with a receipt in it. The boy took it up and glanced at it for a moment, and then put it back down.

"What should we do for dinner?" she asked.

"Are you hungry?"

"A bit. I think I will be soon."

"Good. I'm getting pretty helmet-headed myself, so I think I'd better eat something. Did you know that these exquisite beers are only costing about one and a half dollars, each? Isn't that magnificent?"

Her beer was cold enough going down that it did seem to make her feel really that much better, fresher. It wasn't good beer, but the time and the day and the cold glass made it all a *good* beer. She wondered whether she wouldn't be happier drinking a white wine, her usual beverage, but she let the cold of her glass cool her hand and let the moment wash over her like a fine reward.

"It's been some hot day we've had," he told her. "*Some* day. I'm sorry about all that European Driving business. I understand that if that's not you it wouldn't be too much fun to have me goading you. I'm sorry."

She reached to put her hand on his and he kept his hand where it'd been, on the table. With her thumb, she rubbed along the top edge of his first finger. "I'm sorry," she said. "I shouldn't have yelled at you about it; I just get nervous sometimes when I'm driving and you were actually making me crazy."

"Me?"

"Yes. You were being pretty awful."

"You think so? Me? Awful?"

"I'm sorry." Across the street were two Spanish women sitting across from one another talking. They smoked cigarettes and pecked their heads when they talked so that the effect was that they appeared to move as small birds would; since she couldn't hear them, or wouldn't have understood them if she could, she could almost believe they were some form of tropical bird that she was finding only here in Spain.

"So you think I was a pain in the ass?"

"We can drop this," she said. "It was a hot day and now we're done with that. Let's enjoy our drinks."

"Is there a place you'd like to eat?"

She showed him the card she'd picked up: El Café Henri. "I'd love to just eat tapas tonight. To try real Spanish tapas. Let's just eat that."

"That's cool. Usually when you do something like that you're ordering without knowing any of the prices and you can get burned, but everything seems to be so cheap here that it'll probably be fine; I mean how could you go wrong in *Huesca*?"

She laughed; it was funny. He removed another cigarette from his package and lit it. He was something else entirely on this trip, someone different than the person she knew back home. All he did there, it seemed, was worry about whether he'd gotten enough done, which he never thought he had. It seemed like she could never get him to relax, though she did her best to try. She wasn't sure if it was something wrong with her or wrong with them that he never seemed to calm down, but she thought that if she could get him to relax and ease off, things would be so much better.

"Should we go eat after this drink?" he said, taking a big sip that left only about half of his glass full, and nothing in the bottle.

Walden

Adam Berkman didn't know the right thing to do. He and Corinne had just broken up, something that felt right, but he couldn't be sure.

After a hard year apart, trying to navigate the difficulties of a long-distance relationship, Adam had come back to Boston for the summer break from his MBA classes at Northwestern. They had both come to recognize that spending their summer together was critical. If they never saw each other, what was the point? So Adam moved back to Boston, into Corinne's small apartment where everything was tastefully decorated in light colors. In Chicago, he could have lined up an internship with any of a half-dozen brokerage houses, but in Boston the job-searching went slowly. After two weeks of interviews that led to nothing, he began to realize that spending his days alone in Corinne's apartment, waiting for interviews or for her to come home, was not what he wanted.

They started talking at 5 that morning, after she found him awake in the living room, watching the sunrise. When she came in, Adam didn't look. "I can't do this anymore," he said. "I wish I could, but I can't."

"What's wrong with this?" she asked. "We were going to try."

"I know," he said. "But it's not right. That's the best I can explain. I wish it was another way." On the other side of the street, one of the thin pipes atop a large brick building emitted a trail of steam that rose up into the sky. "I'm sorry."

She called in sick. He wished she wouldn't, asked her not to, but she was crying, hard, and wanted to help him pack his things. Adam left—he had to get out of the apartment; he went to Cambridge to get his mother's car, but Corinne was still there when he got back, which made packing even harder. She refused to do anything but help him, a kindness he could barely endure, and together they turned the morning into a series of crying and ruined goodbyes.

When the car was packed, he went to his mother's. His father was there, waiting to talk to him, to find out what were his plans. Adam told him the relationship had come to a permanent-feeling close, that he felt like he'd finally made an important decision. It felt right, he told his father.

Then, in the late afternoon, Corinne called him. "I've just been laid off," she whispered over the phone. "I don't have a job."

"Jesus," he said, sitting alone in what had once been his bedroom at his mother's, the room where he had once punched a man named Vaughn—a boyfriend of his mother's who Adam had thought she should not date. That decision had ended badly.

Now, he held the phone close to his head and looked at his suitcase on the other side of the room. He closed his eyes. "How did this happen?" he asked.

Walden

"They said they have to make cutbacks," she said. "Jana told me they're laying off six people." She said she wasn't even supposed to show up to work tomorrow; they'd told her today had been her last.

"I thought they had to give you two weeks," he said. He had been back from Chicago for less than a month. "Do you want me to come over?"

She did. "I want to," he said. Of course he should go. He felt guilty for offering in a way that forced her to ask. He would see her, that was what made the most sense; he would go there, set himself aside and go because she needed him. He could push his decisions away for tonight, at least.

He found his parents in the back yard talking, behaving like friends, for once. When Adam told them what'd happened, they couldn't believe it. "That's terrible!" his father said.

"I know. I'm going over there. That's the right thing to do, right?" They shrugged. His father always pushed him to make his own decisions, avoided offering advice. But he knew to go. His mother told him to take the car, even gave him money to spend on dinner. He thought eating something would help, and so he called ahead to order ribs and chicken, the best thing he could think of at a time like this. But he hoped Corinne would eat.

She looked under control when she came down to open the door. He set the bags of food down and hugged her, wrapped her in his arms, and held her shoulders. "It'll all be all right," he said. "Things will turn around. You'll get past this."

When she straightened, he asked her if they should eat in the courtyard, or upstairs in her apartment. She said downstairs was where Jana had told her. "She wasn't sure how to. She told me one of the principals wanted to come, that she had thought to bring Katia, but finally decided to come alone." Adam knew that Jana lived close by, that she and Corinne were friends, went to brunch occasionally. "She just came here and told me they were letting me go."

"And it's effective today?" She wiped her fingers under her eyes, nodding. "What did you say?"

"I told her I just wanted to go upstairs and be alone."

She led him into the elevator. They had ridden in this small compartment many times, holding hands, kissing, even taking each others' clothes off one night, drunk, coming in past midnight. Now they stood apart from one another, and Adam's hands held only white plastic bags of white styrofoam containers.

They got off on her floor and he followed her down the hall, the one he'd been so impressed by the first time he'd seen it. Looking at her welcome mat, the flowered design distinctly hers, he smiled. In her apartment, he could still feel the heavy effects of the day's heat weighing down on them, on the air. It was only July, but the day felt like mid-August.

Adam went out to the apartment's thin balcony, hoping for a breeze, and started setting the food on the small iron table. He brought out the two new folding chairs Corinne had just bought. When he first saw them, he knew two would be unnecessary soon, but he kept quiet because he hadn't wanted to rush. He set the chairs on the sides of the table and started unwrapping the food. They had Cokes, coleslaw, chicken, ribs, macaroni and cheese, candied yams, collard greens. All of it smelled good.

"Eating is a good thing at a time like this," he said. "It can make you feel better, even if only a little." He tasted the macaroni. "Here, this is good," he said. She came to the door and he handed her the container. She looked disinterested, tasted a small bite, and passed it back. Adam could not ignore the ribs and he started eating—he was suddenly very hungry. He was glad to see her come outside and sit down across from him, but she just sat there, looking at the street below. He kept eating, hoping she'd relax, and he was holding a rib, with barbeque sauce all over his hands, when he looked up and saw her crying. He wiped his hands on some napkins and reached for her, but in the awkward folding chair and across the table, he only could manage his hand onto her knee. "Oh, Bear," he said.

She dried her eyes with her fingers. "It's not fair. I've been doing a good job. That's what everyone tells me. Why would they do this?"

"I'm sorry," he said. He wiped his mouth. "Let's go inside. Can we?" He wanted to hold her and let her cry this thing out, for things to be alright. He led her inside and onto the couch, abandoning the food. He sat with his arm across her shoulders. "How did this happen?" he asked. He leaned back and gently guided her down with him, helped her to lie on his chest.

"My father said I should come home," she said, putting her head against his shoulder. "I could hear my mother crying. They both said I should come home. That's their answer."

He touched her hair with his fingers, and put his other arm around her back. "It's a lot to move half way around the world from where you grew up. Maybe it would be nice to go back to Berlin for a while, just to relax and let this thing blow over. You wouldn't have to stay long."

"No," she said. "I'm not ready to do that. Not now." She

leaned into him and then sat up, wiping her face with her hands. He saw the food outside, the bags blowing in the wind, and got up to bring the containers inside. He set them on the coffee table.

"Here," he said, unwrapping the chicken and tasting a bite. "This is good. Try this. I think if you eat something you'll start feeling better."

"It just doesn't feel right to leave. I'm not done living here. There are other U.S. cities I want to try. New York."

"This gives you the chance then, right?" He wrapped the food and put it in the kitchen, washed his hands, and came back to the couch. "Think of this as though you just got two free months to really think about where you want to go next, a summer vacation. You can find a new job, take time to think things over, figure out what you want." She nodded and he worked his hand up her back. He massaged the twin tendons in her neck, feeling their tension, then worked around and down to her shoulder blades and along the sides of her back with both hands.

"Now that I don't have a job I could come with you to Chicago," she said.

He looked out the window and thought of that morning: how he'd felt sitting on the couch, thinking, when he couldn't sleep. The day had moved on, but the buildings across the street, and his feelings, were the same. "I don't know," he said. "Maybe it's still not right for us. Maybe we still have to try something different."

"I know," she said. Her breath evened out, slowed. He handed her the tissues and she blew her nose, then he took her in his arms and lay back again. He held her on his chest, rocking slightly; and she brought her legs up onto the couch.

"This is big, Bear," he said. "But some day you might look back and think how it made you stronger." He listened to her breathe, watching the clouds shift outside her windows. "I know that sounds stupid," he said.

He still loved to hold her. Sometimes at night he had imagined a world where their bed was everything and he could save her from the difficulties of life, just by keeping her there in his arms, but lately it had been just their two bodies on her hard futon, trying to sleep in the heat, her warmth making him uncomfortable. Perhaps it was her metabolism that made her body so hot—she liked her shower water scalding, always said she felt cold. Her body kept their bed warm like an oven.

She slid her fingers along the inside of his forearm and he moved it away from her. In a rush, what had troubled him about their relationship came back to him: it was about simple touches like that one, things he wanted to tell her and couldn't, about how they never seemed completely capable of expressing their feelings to one another. He remembered the time he'd tried to tell her why he didn't like her to touch the soft inside of his wrist and how she'd started crying. He closed his eyes.

"We should do something," he said, helping her up. "Maybe we could go for a walk?" He doubted if anything could make her happy. "We could go to Newbury."

That she sat up and agreed surprised him; she seemed almost pleased, as if going were actually a good idea. Newbury

Street had been a place where they'd eaten fancy dinners the summer before, shopped and bought expensive clothes they thought they could afford. But even then, over nice food, something had seemed wrong to him. Even then.

Now he would drive them to Newbury Street in his mother's car. It would be good to drive; after almost a month of living with Corinne and riding everywhere in her car, he missed feeling in control, even of something so small.

He held her waist as they walked to the elevator and they held hands outside as they walked to the car. "It's hot tonight," he said. "Today was like the first hot humid day of summer, and we made it. You made it. You got through one of the worst days I've ever heard of today. That was a lot, Bear."

She nodded. "I hope you'll always call me that."

"And it's still hot," he said. She had her hand inside the crook of his elbow and he maneuvered his way out to wrap his arm around her back. "We should go swimming. How about we go out to Walden Pond?"

"Really," she said, her face suddenly bright. She turned toward him, took both of his hands. "Can we?"

He knew how difficult it would be to go: it was a long drive that cooled you off as you drove there, the water was always cold, and sneaking in could be difficult—but now they had to try it. She was as happy as he'd seen her all night. "Let's go, then," he said. "Let's drive out there."

She was smiling now. "Okay," she said. "Good. We're going to Walden Pond."

At a small sidewalk café outside her apartment, a trio played jazz. Adam noticed a young couple with short dreadlocks sitting on a nearby wooden bench, listening. Their arms were intertwined and they held hands, each of them tapping out time to the music with their feet. There were other couples sitting at the café's fancy tables, but these two sat apart, quietly enjoying the night, smiling, not worried about how they appeared to the others. They seemed happy, and Adam envied them this. He wondered how they had come to find one another or what it took to feel comfortable like that, a way he had never felt with Corinne, with anyone.

He opened her door at the car, glad to be helping, doing something for her after the two full months of her helping him. He wanted to do something which could make her feel better, that was all he wanted, to do this for her, help her to end this night. As they drove along the Charles, he saw the familiar sights he had always loved: the Boston skyline, the Citgo sign, the fancy Bay Back apartments with the big windows that you could see into—the ones he imagined owning some day, looking out of onto the river and Storrow Drive. He was glad he had come home to try living with her: nothing had been lost, he reasoned, and now he could say he had given it a legitimate try.

She stayed quiet until they got to the highway, then, with trees on both sides, she spoke of growing up in Germany, how beautiful the mountains and the forests were there. She told him that these suburbs outside of Boston, their tree-covered rolling hills and the nice cars, reminded her of home. And he knew that he still loved her. It pained him as he listened to her voice, as she held his hand. He wanted to do anything to help her get over this even though he knew the water in the pond would be cold.

In Concord, he checked the front gate and found it locked as he'd expected, but there were a few cars parked by the

Thoreau Gift Shop. He couldn't remember if he'd ever seen cars there at night before. But there they were. If someone watched these spots they might ticket him, or worse, but probably wouldn't tow—he hoped not.

"Do you think it'd be all right for us to park here?" he asked.

"I don't know. We won't be long, will we?"

"No," he said. "You're right."

He parked and locked his door, then went around to her side. She was still inside, looking through her purse, and he tapped on her window. "We should go," he said. "It'd be bad if anyone saw us here." He looked at the other cars to see if any of them had a common identifier, any sign of some group designation, but none did. The car next to his was a station wagon with Missouri plates, a road atlas spread across the front seat, two sleeping bags in the back.

The air was much cooler and less thick than in the city here; the humidity was gone—the trees and the pond seemed to cool everything—but Adam had the air-conditioning off and the windows closed on the ride out, so they were still sticky from the city, warm enough to swim.

"It's so nice here," she said.

He took her hand and led her toward the entrance. It was dark and the quiet of the empty forest brought back its familiar spookiness. They crouched under the gate, going separately, but rejoined hands after, at the top of the downhill slope of a road. They climbed down, passing under trees in darkness, and emerged onto a beach lit by the moonlight. "It's wonderful," she said, walking to the water, bending to feel it. "And so warm."

He directed her to a trail that led to the more secluded spots farther along the shoreline. At the trailhead trees crowded in on both sides, the heavy forest sloping above, dark and full of sounds, and a thin line of pines between them and the pond. He could hear the sound of water lapping gently against the shore.

She walked ahead, taking the trail like she knew it, as he held back, keeping track of the wire fence that protected the shore, looking for an opening where they could swim. "The air is so clear and clean here," she said.

In a few minutes, his eyes had adjusted to the darkness, but he could not see the water when he heard a panting, splashing sound ahead of them, and he grabbed her hand. "Shhh. There's something there," he said. If it was an animal, he didn't want it to surprise them, but he didn't want to surprise it either. He went ahead of her, slowly, feeling along the wire, chilled by the oddness of this sound. In the dark, his imagination always convinced him that sounds were made by creatures. Some thing must be in the water.

"I think it's—" and she started laughing.

At a break in the fence, he saw steps leading down to the water with people's clothes set in piles. He realized that he'd heard a woman. She was just getting used to the cold water, breathing hard and splashing around. Corinne laughed. "It's all right here, Adam," she said, walking ahead again. "Don't be afraid."

As he followed, he felt along the fence for another break, hoping to find an empty set of steps to the water. They followed the path as it wrapped around a long bend of shoreline, approaching the far beaches he liked to come to in the summer. And then, when he found the next gap in the fence, the dark stones leading down were empty of clothes and they were separated from the other people by the bend; no one else was around. He saw water splashing against the shore. "This is our spot," he said.

She stopped, leaning forward to see, and said, "Perfect."

He stepped down and took her hand to help her down. He wanted to sweep her legs into his arms and carry her, but he didn't, knew he would never do something like that here, that if he fell while carrying her down the steep stones they'd both be badly hurt. Instead, he took each step ahead of her and held her hand as she lowered herself behind him.

Tonight she wore the old clothes that'd been his favorite those first long weekends after he'd met her at his cousin's wedding, when he flew in for visits: her long blue skirt fanned out around her feet, his favorite Nikes, and her tank top that fit her as tightly as anything she owned. She held the skirt above her knees with one hand so she could step freely down the stairs, and he saw her legs from her small blue sneakers up—her legs that were always perfectly shaven. He wanted to touch them, to run his fingers along her smooth calves. But instead he lowered himself down the steps to where only the pond was below him. Careful to hold her arm until her feet were steady, he sat and hugged her legs, feeling her shin with his fingers. "What do you think, Bear?"

"It's beautiful here. The pond, its ripples, and the moon's reflection, all the stars. It's so wonderful."

"Yeah," he said. "I hope the water's not too cold."

"You're so grumpy," she said. "You've always been sad."

He placed his shoes on the step above him, took his shirt

off, and stretched his toes to the water. It was cold, but he tried saying, "It's not so bad." They had come this far. "I've been here at night before," he said, "But always later in the summer. There haven't been that many warm days yet."

He slid off the rock, into the shallow water, and landed on soft sand. "Yow," he said. "It's pretty cold."

"You're not going to swim in your shorts, are you?" she asked.

He looked down at himself, even knowing already that he still had shorts on. "No," he said. "I was just feeling the water." He heard the people they'd passed, the gentle splashing of the man and the woman, but he couldn't see any movement or shapes along the shoreline in the dark. He unbuttoned his shorts and, careful not to lose his wallet or keys, stepped out of them one leg at a time, holding them above the water.

She touched his shoulder, steadying herself for balance as she removed her shoes.

He folded his shorts and put them on the step next to her, naked in an unfamiliar, unembarrassed way. His penis stood out below his stomach, but he was not ashamed of how the moonlight revealed it. The water cold on his ankles, he was here, with her, and for the first time everything seemed fine. He told himself everything was fine.

She stood above him in the moonlight and slipped out of her skirt. Her body looked as beautiful as he'd ever seen her, her legs long and pale, a simple white thong, which she slipped down over her feet, onto the stones. When she pulled the top over her head, her nipples pointed in the cold. He saw the simple flatness of her stomach, thought how her body was as perfect as any he'd ever known, with a realness that was fully human—she had bones under her skin. He stood below her, beholding the simple beauty of the pond and the trees around them, and her bright pale form above him. She shone in the moonlight, illuminated as if the moon for that moment had focused its brilliance on her. She stood no less than three feet above him, nude, shining. The shadow of a tree branch cut across her side. He followed its curve to her breast with his eyes, thinking as if his gaze were his fingers. He passed over her shoulders, along the line of her collar bone, and up her white neck. When he came to her eyes, she smiled as if she knew the moon had caught her this way, given her such light.

"We're at Walden Pond," she said and laughed.

He heard the wind and felt a cold gust prickling the hair on his legs, making his skin tighter. After a chill ran through him, he touched her leg, felt its smoothness. She giggled. "You're beautiful," he said. He held his hand up for her to take it and when she did he steadied her and she bent down to step into the water. "It's only sand here," he said. "Don't worry."

As she crouched and slipped her leg down, she laughed at the touch of the cold on her toes, squeezed his hand. When her left foot fell onto the sand, she slipped slightly so that she landed suddenly with both feet in the water, both of her hands on his shoulders to steady herself. "Ha. It's not so bad, then," she said. "This can be our baptism. Where we wash it all away and start fresh, promising ourselves that from here on nothing bad will happen to us. That we'll wash it all away and leave only the best things."

"But some of what happened today won't change." He was sorry as soon as he'd said it, but he wanted everything to remain clear.

"I know," she said. "But this will clean us, this can change something, even if only for us as separate people." She caught her breath as the water hit her thighs. "Only good things will happen after this for us. Let's promise." Her voice was soft. She put her hand on his arm and he noticed her eyes were closed. "We can wash away the bad luck and whatever is hard, and come to something new."

"OK," he said. She led him out into the cold water. "I promise," he told her, stepping forward, wading deeper until the water reached his shins, then his knees and—too quickly, it seemed—the tops of his thighs. The water was clean and cold, pure. "You deserve good things," he said. "They'll come to you."

"We're washing everything bad away."

His penis seemed to be floating above the pond, standing erect on its own. She looked at it and smiled. "I see you," she said, and reached out to touch him.

He stepped forward. "Co-o-o-ld," he said. "This is where it hurts."

He stepped into deeper water, breathing like a Lamaze pupil, fighting the shock. She laughed. "You're brave." He raised his hand to splash her, but realized how out of the question that was—an act for a summer day, with the sun hot on their skin.

Now he led her deeper, until he was in to his sternum and she to her shoulders, and she was shivering, shaking in the water. She swam in front of him and stood against his chest, her teeth chattering, their bodies together. When he touched her shoulder, she shied away, but then held him when he took her in his arms. He ran his hand along her legs, feeling the goosebumps on her skin, and brought them up, around his waist. He felt surprise at how warm her body seemed against his; she was warmer than him, warmed him in the cold water. He held his arms along the backs of her thighs, supporting her as she grasped him by the shoulders, her legs around his waist.

"It's so cold," she said, her hair wet against his neck.

"You're keeping me warm, Bear. Your oven."

She kissed his neck and her lips were cold, but she'd stopped shivering. He pressed her against him and carried her out until the water was at his neck—where only his feet could touch the bottom—and he did not feel cold.

"We're in," she said. "We made it."

"Because of you."

She kissed his forehead and his temple; their lips met and he could feel hers cold and soft, moving as she told him she loved him, and then they finally kissed, the tip of her tongue warm between his lips. Her legs had smoothed but her nipples stood erect against his chest. He nuzzled his face into her shoulder, holding her tight to his chest for her warmth, squeezing her.

The cold water occurred to him as if it was only a fact now; he discerned its clean film against him, but she staved off his feeling the cold.

"We're clean," she said.

The moon and the big dipper hung above them; the trees along the opposite shore reflecting darkness against the still water of the pond. He felt held: by her, by the water, and as if the crispness had done something to him, something he could not explain. He wondered how many more times he would hold her body, if he ever would again, and he thought about times he'd held her: in a hotel room on a vacation in Barcelona, after she'd flown all night to see him; the night after his grandmother died, when he'd counted the beating of their hearts; and after their first time together, when he peeked under the covers and secretly looked at her body in awe.

Then, from somewhere in the world beyond the trees, he heard the rumble and the whistle of a train coming, and soon he saw the lights and the cars themselves skirting along the top edge of the pond, just behind the tree-line in the woods. He turned so she could see it. "It's a train," he said.

It was headed away from them, on a tangent to their lives, taking strangers to their homes in the night—places he might never see, places inhabited by people he'd never know. He wondered if, by pointing it out to her, he had made her aware of the train and its existence in the world.

It rattled on its tracks, a line of a dozen passenger cars knocking along in the night. The rush of it speeding away toward destinations he would never take her to—places he would have to explore on his own—this chilled him. He couldn't move until the train was gone. Then, when it had passed, they stood on his legs and listened. Her body felt clean and smooth, still perfect. She held her lips cold against his neck, and the wet ends of her hair brushed his cheek. She squeezed herself against his body. He smoothed her hair back, cupping her head in his hands.

He kissed her then, felt the cold slipperiness of her lips and the sharpness of her tongue moving against his. Her eyelashes tickled his cheeks. Her lips were dark from the cold, as beautiful as he'd ever see them. She looked cleaned, cleansed, and he believed it, believed in her, seeing the purity in her face. They kissed again, and, though he knew it was time to go, he held her more tightly. He felt the protection of her legs around him and her warmth against his chest, the comfort from the cold that he'd never expected, and he knew: he knew what it would mean to be alone.